mon

DEATH AT
BRIAR RIDGE

DEATH AT BRIAR RIDGE

•

A Reverend Harvey Ashe Mystery

CHARLES M. POORE

AVALON BOOKS
THOMAS BOUREGY AND COMPANY, INC.
401 LAFAYETTE STREET
NEW YORK, NEW YORK 10003

PRINTED IN THE UNITED STATES OF AMERICA
ON ACID-FREE PAPER
BY HADDON CRAFTSMEN, BLOOMSBURG, PENNSYLVANIA

For Debra, who believed

Acknowledgments

I wish to give all honor to the Lord Jesus Christ, who made this work possible. Apart from Him, I can do nothing. He gives good gifts to His children.

Also, I wish to give special thanks to my ninth-grade English teacher, Mrs. Jeanne Koone. Mrs. Koone offered praise and encouragement at a time when I needed it most. I would never have persevered without her urging.

Chapter One

Reverend Harvey Ashe opened the front door of his modest three-bedroom home. As he stepped out onto the brick stoop a gust of arctic wind met him in the face. It sent a chill through his body. Harvey shivered a moment as he buttoned his heavy coat, and began walking down the slate walkway.

The neighborhood was quiet on this wintry January weekday. There were no children laughing, no dogs barking. There was only the steady swish of wind swirling through the barren hardwoods. It had been an unusually frigid winter for the southeastern piedmont.

Harvey looked up through the bony limbs of a huge oak in his front yard, its roots causing the walkway to bulge. He saw heavy gray clouds lumbering across a frozen sky. He opened the redwood-stained picket gate.

Harvey pulled the collar of his coat up over his face, and reached out to open the red brick mailbox. The inside of the box felt strangely warm compared to the open air. He produced a couple of bills, a letter, and the latest advertisement from the local drugstore. Large yellow letters on the front of the ad proclaimed microwave popcorn on sale, four packs for a dollar! Harvey knew he would be stopping by there to stock up.

Just then a large truck roared by, and a moment later the tumultuous wind hit him as if it were a solid object. Harvey turned and trotted back toward the house.

"Close that door, Harvey!" called Sarah Ashe from the chair by the fireplace. The large cat curled up in Sarah's lap squinted at the light from the open door. Harvey pushed the door closed against the relentless wind, pulling off his coat as he did so.

"It's all right, Muffin," said Sarah to the cat as she gently stroked the silky gray fur. "You go back to sleep. Daddy won't open that old door again." Muffin purred audibly.

"Sorry, honey," he said as he walked quickly to the fireplace and put his frozen hands to the heat. "It's getting colder out there; must be below twenty by now."

Sarah put down her novel. "What did we get in the mail?"

Harvey handed the mail to her as he rubbed his thawing fingers in the warmth. As the fire crackled, Harvey felt the gentle rubbing of something against his leg. He looked down to see a small tabby kitten meowing softly and looking up at him. Large green eyes gazed into his.

"Ulysses!" Harvey said as he reached down to scratch behind its ears. "You like being next to that fire, don't you?"

The kitten meowed again as if to answer him. As Sarah flipped through the drugstore ad, Harvey smiled at her, grateful for such a woman as she. At forty-five, Sarah was still more beautiful than many women of twenty. Her soft hair was just beginning to show a few strands of shimmering silver. Her skin was still smooth and her smile was radiant. Wise and strong in faith, she still sported a sense of humor that made it difficult for Harvey to ever be angry with her. She had stood solidly beside Harvey through the most difficult days of his early adulthood. She stayed when she really didn't have to, when she could have had any man she wanted. Back then, Harvey was away most of the time, busting drug pushers, cleaning up after senseless murders, and chasing pimps through all hours of the night. He hated the very memory of those big-city cop days.

But things had worked out well after all. Sarah had stayed, raising three wonderful children, mostly by herself. Then Harvey felt called to the ministry. And for twelve years, since his graduation from seminary college at thirty-five, Harvey had been chasing souls instead of criminals. He pastored the small Baptist church in the quiet town of Laurel Springs, Georgia, at the foot of Briar Ridge Mountain. Harvey and Sarah had moved there only two years ago. Harvey hoped this would be the place he lived out all of his remaining years.

Unlike Sarah, the years had hardened the Reverend's features, and his age showed. His face was weathered, more like a soldier than a country preacher. His hair was getting gray like the winter sky, his bristly mustache still showing remnants of the black hair he once knew. His build was still muscular and fit, as the old cop inside demanded. Despite his tough exterior, Harvey's heart had been softened over the years by his ministry and the love of his lifelong companion. Though Harvey would never admit it, Ulysses found plenty of room in his heart as well. Harvey's life was a little sliver of paradise on earth.

Sarah shuffled through the bills.

"Here's a letter from John Galen," she said, tearing open the envelope. "I wonder what he could be writing to me about?"

"Maybe he's planning another one of those carnivals in the craft village this spring, like he did three years ago," theorized Harvey.

"Oh, I hope not. That whole thing was such a mess, and a distraction to the craft shops. People come there for the country atmosphere, not to play ring toss and goofy golf. They can do that at the county fair.''

Sarah stopped her sermon to read the letter, despite Muffin's pawing at the paper:

Dear Mrs. Ashe,

As President of the Briar Ridge Craft Village Owners Association, we respectfully request your presence at an important meeting to be held next Sunday evening at the Briar Ridge Lodge. Meals and overnight lodging will be provided, and spouses are invited. There will be a very important announcement concerning the Lodge, and all interested parties are urged to attend. RSVP.

> *Sincerely,*
> *John Galen*
> *Proprietor, Briar Ridge Lodge*

''What on earth could this be about, Harvey?'' asked Sarah.

''Call John, tell him we'll come, and you'll find out.''

Harvey opened the gas bill, fearing what numbers the cold January had generated. Sarah gazed into the fire, still holding the letter out of Muffin's reach.

''It would be nice to have a weekend at the Lodge

together,'' she said. ''We haven't stayed there since our anniversary a year ago.''

''You're there every weekend during the tourist season, dear.''

''That's work, Harvey. I mean to relax and enjoy the rest.''

''Well, I'd love to go, especially if John Galen is actually giving us a free weekend. He never gave away anything free in his life. Why don't you call him?''

''Why, Reverend,'' Sarah said with a wink, ''are you trying to entice me to go off with you to some lonely mountain retreat?''

Harvey looked deep into her still-youthful eyes as Muffin succeeded in chewing the corner of the letter. He smiled and said, ''With no one else, dear.''

''Daddy, how are you going to survive this weekend without your baby?'' said Laura Pace as she took the cat carrier from Harvey. Laura and Sarah laughed as they entered the little house.

''It's not my *baby*,'' disputed Harvey, ''it's just a cat.''

Sarah laughed again as she set down the other carrier containing a loudly protesting Muffin.

''Your father contends that getting Ulysses was only for my benefit. But you've seen how he's wrapped around that little kitten's paw.''

Harvey had opened the cat carrier and was cradling Ulysses as if he were a human baby. The kitten purred softly as Harvey scratched under his chin. Harvey seemed oblivious to his wife's comments.

"That's right," Harvey said to the kitten, "you're just a cat, and nothing more." Ulysses blinked.

"I don't think Daddy gave me that much attention when I was a baby," said Laura, taking Ulysses from Harvey's arms. "I guess I just wasn't as cute."

Sarah shook her head. "No, dear. You got more attention and love than either of these cats, believe me!"

Harvey's son-in-law, Timothy Pace, walked into the foyer from the den, coffee cup in hand. Harvey thought him to be a painfully young CPA, with sandy blond hair that gave him the look of a surfer. He had married Harvey's daughter just three months ago.

"Hi, Mr. Ashe," he said exuberantly. "I'm glad you guys are getting away for the weekend. I know how hard you've been working recently."

"Please, Timothy," said Harvey. "I've been your father-in-law for three months now. I think it's safe to call me something other than 'Mr. Ashe.' It makes me feel like an old man. 'Dad' will do."

"Okay . . . Dad . . . it's just hard to get used to, you know?"

"Yes, I can imagine."

Timothy held up his mug. "Care for a cup of coffee?"

"No, Timothy, we've really got to be getting along. I want to get up that mountain before dark."

''What?'' Timothy looked astonished. ''A Baptist preacher turning down a cup of coffee? I must be imagining all this.''

Harvey laughed. ''I know it must seem heretical, but I don't see well in the dark, you know. I wish we could stay longer; maybe we will on the way back when we pick up the babies . . . I mean, the cats.''

Sarah laughed and rolled her eyes as if exasperated. ''What will we ever do with your father?''

Laura moved over to Harvey and put her arms around his waist, squeezing hard.

''Just take care of him, Mom.''

''Don't I always?'' Sarah nudged Harvey's arm. Feeling hopelessly outnumbered, Harvey turned toward the front door.

''Well, we'd better be on our way,'' Harvey said. ''Thanks again, honey, for keeping the cats while we're gone. We'll see you Monday morning.''

Harvey and Sarah exchanged kisses with their daughter, and Harvey extended a firm handshake with Timothy. Timothy tried to squeeze just a bit harder than Harvey, but was unable to. Harvey had the firmest handshake in Laurel Springs, maybe even the county.

''You know,'' Sarah said as they sat down in the car, ''I'm so thankful that Laura met such a fine, upstanding man while she was in school. He's really wonderful, isn't he?''

Harvey cranked the engine into life. "Yeah, I'll have him straightened out in no time."

A light snow began to fall on the shiny black Cadillac crawling steadily up the narrow winding road leading to Briar Ridge Lodge. To the left of the road rose steep forested slopes, interrupted by occasional outcroppings of granite. To the right were sheer hundred-foot drops, protected by a guardrail marred by dents and scrapes from past mishaps. As the elevations approached thousands of feet, the Cadillac penetrated a dense level of fog.

Harvey Ashe slowed the car to about twenty-five miles per hour. Feeling a chill as the fog surrounded the car, he reached for the climate control dial on the gray dashboard. He moved it up a couple of degrees. A layer of warmth rose slowly from the floorboard a few moments later. Harvey took a deep, relaxing breath.

Sarah, however, was sitting straight up in the seat, eyes wide and every muscle tensed. Her fingernails dug firmly into the velour armrest. Harvey let his large hand slide discreetly onto Sarah's clenched one. His thumb caressed hers.

"Relax, Sarah," he assured with his soft, understanding counselor's voice. "We're almost there."

Sarah sighed quickly and harshly. "I know, darling. I just hate to drive in weather like this. You can't see twenty feet ahead of you for the fog, with sheer cliffs just one careless move away.''

"Hon, have you ever known me to be careless?''

Sarah thought for a moment, remembering all the times her husband had left the oven on all night, or gone to bed while the fireplace logs still burning. Then she smiled.

"No, dear, I guess you're right,'' she said. "You've never been careless.

Harvey smiled in small triumph as Sarah reached up and turned the climate control knob down two degrees.

"It was nice of the Deacon Board to give you a week's vacation on such short notice, wasn't it?'' commented Sarah.

"Well, I hadn't had a weekend off in a long time. They owed it to me. Besides, Jason will do a fine job in the pulpit. As young as he is, he's already a better preacher than this old dog.''

"In his dreams, maybe. He's all book knowledge and no real people skills if you ask me. He's got a lot to learn.''

"Perhaps,'' Harvey mused as he inched the climate control up a degree, "but he's got a good start. Keep your eye on that boy, I say.''

"I'd rather keep my eye on you!''

Harvey chuckled.

*   *   *

One last arduous climb was behind them, and the Briar Ridge Lodge began to materialize in the fog. The snow was coming harder as the car turned in the drive and gracefully slid into a parking space. They parked beside a mint condition 1968 Camaro Z-28, with Nevada plates. It was fire-engine red with black racing stripes, front and rear spoilers, and raised white letter tires. The air above its hood rippled as the heat from its still-hot engine rose. The car simply glowed in the grayness of its surroundings.

"Would you look at that!" Harvey's eyes suddenly were sixteen years old again. He remembered those carefree hot-rodding days when gas was forty cents a gallon, and nobody really cared what kind of mileage a car got.

"Put your eyes back in their sockets, Harvey," said Sarah. "That car would know better than to let you get near it."

"They don't make cars like that anymore. I'll bet the engine's a '396!"

"A what?"

"Oh, I'm sorry, dear, these days it would be a six-liter." Harvey still admired the car, as if forgetting why he was there. "I wonder who it belongs to?"

"Well, let's go in and we'll probably find out."

Harvey laughed. "Okay, I get the message. Time to start acting like the wise old clergyman on vacation again."

Harvey opened his door. The air was damp and

cold; snow was gently blowing into his hair. As he opened the truck to get the baggage he looked around the parking lot and saw only a few cars.

Sarah opened her door and stood up, stretching in the cold air. She picked up one suitcase, Harvey the other one, and they walked hand in hand down the rock stairs. They passed beds of azalea bushes devoid of flowers and covered with a light dusting of snow. Finally they were standing at the large oak doors.

The lodge itself was built in the style of a great rustic ranch, with three stories and a myriad of gables looking out from the top level. The lodge was right on the top of the mountain overlooking what in the springtime was a breathtaking view of the valley below.

Harvey opened the door and they stepped into the cozy lobby. A homey warmth enwrapped them. They put their suitcases down by the front desk. The lobby had hardwood floors with old-fashioned area rugs. The furniture was Early American with large throw pillows, some with handmade cross-stitch patterns. There were grand landscape paintings hanging majestically on paneled walls. The lighting was from occasional table lamps rather than harsh overheads. The front desk was decorated in rough cedar paneling, except for the countertop itself, which was finely varnished and shining with the light from a small desk lamp next to the cash register.

The desk clerk was helping a stylishly dressed guest

who had arrived just before Harvey and Sarah. He was a slim man, in his early thirties with thinning brown hair. He wore a navy blue business suit with a bright red tie, and carried a genuine leather attaché. A suit carrier was draped across his arm. He had the unmistakable air of a man who was genuinely wealthy, rather than just trying to appear so.

"Excuse me," said Harvey, "is that your Camaro out there?"

"Yes, it is," replied the man.

"I'm Harvey Ashe," he said, extending his hand. "I couldn't help noticing the car. It's beautiful."

"I'm Scott Grey," the man said, taking Harvey's hand and wincing slightly at the unexpected pressure of his grip. "I saw the car in a show in Phoenix. When I saw that it was for sale, well, I couldn't resist it. I had one similar to it as a teenager, you see, but not quite as nice as that one."

"You were lucky to find it."

"Not really, Mr. Ashe; it's not a particularly rare model. But it does have sentimental meaning to me."

"Of that I'm sure. Does it have a '396?"

"Of course," Grey said, retrieving an American Express Gold Card from the desk clerk along with a room key. "Now if you'll excuse me, I've had a long drive."

"Certainly, Mr. Grey, it's been a pleasure."

Grey nodded an acknowledgment without a smile, and headed up the curved staircase toward the rooms.

"Hi, I'm Lisa Aames, may I help you?" cheerfully asked the desk clerk as Harvey stepped up to the counter.

"Yes, I'm Harvey Ashe, and my wife, Sarah. We're expected."

"Oh yes, Reverend Ashe, we have your room ready. Hi, Sarah, I didn't see you when you first came in. It's good to finally meet your husband."

Harvey smiled diplomatically.

"If you'll just sign the register, Reverend, I'll get your key."

"Thank you," said Harvey as he picked up a pen and began to sign. Lisa reached her thin hand under the counter and picked up a large glass of water. She took a gulp while she waited for Harvey to finish.

"Have you and your mother been feeling well, Lisa?"

"Oh, yes, ma'am, we're doing quite well."

Sarah could tell she was lying tactfully about herself. Lisa did not look well at all. Always a thin and frail redhead, she seemed tired and on edge. Her hands were nervously making unnecessary gestures as she spoke. It did not appear she had had much rest in recent days.

"I'm glad to hear that, Lisa," Sarah replied, not wishing to openly contradict her statement. Lisa could see the motherly concern in Sarah's eyes. She knew the pastor's wife would corner her eventually and find out the truth.

"Reverend Ashe!" came a boisterous voice from an office to the right of the front desk. Harvey looked up to see the Lodge's owner, John Galen, walking toward him with an outstretched hand. Galen was a tall, husky man in his forties, with a bushy beard that was not very well trimmed. He wore blue jeans and a flannel shirt. The hardwood floor shook as he walked.

"Mr. Galen," Harvey replied, shaking his hand, realizing that perhaps he'd met his handshaking match. "Thank you for the invitation; I've looked forward to it."

"I'm so glad that you and Mrs. Ashe could come."

Galen gently took Sarah's hand, and offered a modest smile.

"Mr. Galen," asked Sarah, "just what is all this about? Who else is coming? Is there some kind of trouble?"

"I'd rather just explain once, at the meeting tonight, Mrs. Ashe. I know you must be curious—everyone is. But when you hear, I think you'll understand why I called the meeting. I only ask you to be patient. Come down for dinner at seven o'clock. We are going to set up the private dining room for the meeting. It'll be much more intimate."

"Do you still have any guests other than our group?"

"No, last weekend was the last of the season. We kept a skeleton crew on for just this weekend, then we close for the winter."

"We'll be there," assured Harvey, "and thanks again for the invitation."

"Enjoy it, Reverend!"

At that, Galen returned to his office. Harvey heard the chattering of women's voices closing in behind him. He turned to see Jessica Barrow, the assistant manager, talking in a steady stream to an attractive young blond.

"Sarah!" Jessica called when she saw the Ashes. "So good to see you. I don't think you've been up the mountain in months."

"It's good to see you too, Jessica," replied Sarah.

"Sarah, I'd like you to meet Helen Roma," said Jessica.

Sarah extended her hand. "Pleased to meet you, Helen. This is my husband, Harvey Ashe."

Helen also shook Harvey's hand. As he gently grasped it, he could see the large diamond engagement ring on her finger. Noticing that Harvey had seen it, she smiled shyly. "I'm John Galen's fiancée," she explained. "I'm glad to meet both of you."

"Reverend Ashe is the local Baptist pastor, down in Laurel Springs," said Jessica. "So stay away from him—he's a bad influence!"

Helen looked embarrassed at the joke, but everyone else laughed, including Harvey. He was used to preacher jokes.

"I trust you'll be joining us for dinner tonight?" asked Sarah.

"Of course."

"We're looking forward to it," said Harvey. "We'll see you at dinner, then."

Harvey had their room key and was picking up the luggage when he heard Galen's loud voice booming from his office.

"Helen!" Galen called. "Please come in here for a minute, will you?"

"Excuse me," Helen said. "I have to go."

Harvey and Sarah nodded as they headed upstairs. Helen sheepishly reported to Galen's office as Jessica took her place behind the counter.

"Meek and obedient little lamb, isn't she?" said Sarah as they reached the top of the stairs.

"Just like you?" replied Harvey.

"A regular Proverbs 31 woman. Knowing John Galen, I wonder if she'll be happy."

As they approached the door to their room, Harvey put the key in the lock. "I'm sure John will be happy, as long as she stays meek and obedient!" Harvey grinned as he opened the door.

As the hours passed, the snow continued to fall. Heavy clouds rolled in to blanket the mountain range. The wind was fierce and relentless.

Harvey and Sarah walked down the staircase at about 6:50. At the bottom landing they could see Lisa Aames coming up the stairs, just finishing a conversation.

"No, I can stay overnight, it's no problem," Lisa said to someone. "Okay, eight, I won't forget."

At that, Lisa began up the stairs, meeting Harvey and Sarah on their way down.

"I'm sorry, Miss Aames," Harvey said as he stopped. "I couldn't help but overhear. I hope our meeting tonight isn't causing you to have to work late."

"Oh no, Reverend," assured the bubbly twenty-year-old. "I'm finished for the day. It's just that the road to the Lodge has been closed. The weather's gotten worse, you know."

"No, I didn't," said Harvey.

"Yes, the radio says over a foot of accumulation is expected within twenty-four hours. They may have to plow the road once the snow stops. But I don't mind staying. It gets pretty boring at home with Mother."

Lisa seemed excited about the prospect of spending a night away from home.

"I understand," said Harvey as he continued downstairs. "See you in the morning."

"Good night, Reverend," said Lisa, trotting up the stairs.

Harvey and Sarah entered the now-empty lobby. They stopped at the archway leading to the dining room, next to the sign that read *Please Wait for Hostess*. The rustic dining room seemed enormous because of its emptiness. Massive exposed-wood beams hung over the room. A rock fireplace on the inside wall was blazing. Before the fireplace were several parlor couches and chairs, and a coffee table. A baby grand piano was in one corner, and the outside wall consisted of windows overlooking the valley. Right now, all that could be seen was the snow darting through the lights from the lodge.

Seemingly from nowhere, a smartly dressed, businesslike Jessica Barrow approached them, carrying menus.

"Jessica," said Sarah in surprise, "are you waiting tables tonight?"

"This time of year," replied Jessica as she motioned for them to follow her, "we operate only a skeleton crew. It's just Lisa, the chef, myself, and Mr. Galen . . . oh, and a domestic. She went home early, though. We all chip in with whatever needs to be done. We go on full staff again in April."

"Will you be joining us for dinner?" asked Harvey.

"Eventually, once all the work is done. It shouldn't take long since there's only our party."

As they entered the private room, Harvey could hear boisterous laughter. He recognized Mayor Robert Halon, and Jim Mast from the Chamber of Commerce. Someone had obviously told a joke of questionable taste, and their faces suddenly became serious at the sight of the Reverend.

"Mr. Mayor," said Harvey as he held Sarah's chair for her. "Mr. Mast, good to see you. I see the guest list is quite distinguished, for a little town like Laurel Springs, anyway.''

''Reverend,'' replied Mayor Halon, ''didn't expect to see you here on the weekend.''

''Well, I do have an assistant pastor now,'' explained Harvey, ''so I do get to go on vacation once in a while. But then, you wouldn't have known that unless you'd been to church this month.''

The mayor laughed. ''I know, Reverend, no Sunday school pin for me. Running a town takes all your time, right, Jim?''

Jim Mast nodded affirmatively as he crunched a bread stick. Harvey grinned at the shallow remark as best he could.

Jessica Barrow's stern voice approached again. This time, she seated Benjamin Barten, a local attorney. He, too, seemed surprised at Harvey's presence. Barten exchanged casual greetings with everyone, but didn't enter into conversation. He had always been a quiet sort, speaking only when necessary. Tonight, however, he seemed more preoccupied than normal.

The next to arrive was Helen Roma, who sat in the chair by the head of the table. She was also strangely quiet, sitting silently with her hands in her lap. She was looking down at her place setting, oblivious to the conversation.

Harvey regarded her with curiosity, wondering why she was so suddenly glum. Perhaps she didn't feel good, and the inclement weather was getting her down.

"Harvey," said Sarah.

"Yes, dear . . ."

"Is it cold in here to you?" Sarah was rubbing her arms briskly.

Harvey looked with surprise. "It's not like you to be cold. Are you sick?"

"I don't feel sick, dear, but I haven't felt warm since we arrived. It's just cold in here to me. I think the temperature is dropping."

Harvey looked out the window, and saw the fiercely driving snow.

"I think you're right," Harvey said. "Maybe they'll turn the heat up in a few minutes. Do you want me to run upstairs and get your sweater? You left it on the bed."

"Would you mind, honey?"

Harvey grinned. "I know you'll make it worth my while."

Sarah winked at him as he excused himself. He went back through the main dining room, which was now almost empty. As he entered the lobby, he could hear laughter coming from Galen's office. Harvey didn't want to appear nosy, but he couldn't help turning his head toward the noise. Just as he started up the stairs, he saw an attractive young woman with brown hair coming out of Galen's office. She stopped laughing when she saw Harvey, and continued toward the dining room.

A few minutes later, Harvey returned to the dining room with his wife's sweater. By then, John Galen was there, seated at the head of the table. Helen Roma still sat dourly on his right. To his left sat the gorgeous brunette that Harvey had seen in Galen's office. The lady was casually holding the hand of the attorney, Benjamin Barten.

In the chair next to Harvey's sat Scott Grey. He seemed uncomfortable, as if he felt out of place. Harvey thought he might be worried about something.

Jessica was still busy bringing food to the table, assisted by the chef. When she got through, she sat next to Barten.

The meal consisted of prime rib, the best Harvey remembered having in a long time. The accompanying salad was crisp and everyone seemed to enjoy the hot bread. That is, everyone except Helen. She did not appear to even be aware of the conversation around her. All were eating heartily, and conversation seemed to cover every subject except the one on everyone's mind. As the dinner drew to a close, Galen finally changed the subject.

''I know that everyone's anxious about why I've invited you here,'' he began as the room was suddenly silent, every eye focused on Galen.

''I have an announcement to make concerning the Lodge that will affect each of you in some way. I wanted you to hear it from me first.'' Galen paused and looked around the table, seeming to take note of the expression on each face.

The roar of the wind could be heard outside. Harvey could see snowdrifts collecting on an embankment outside the window.

''I have made a decision,'' said Galen somberly, ''to sell the Briar Ridge Lodge.''

The room was no longer quiet as the air filled with whispers between the guests.

''Some of you have met Scott Grey,'' continued Galen, motioning toward him. ''He is a real estate developer from Las Vegas. He has made a very generous offer for the property. I could hardly refuse. The Lodge has been a very important part of my life, but in recent years the strain of running the place has become burdensome. I'm afraid I'm at the age when I must begin thinking about my retirement years. Mr. Grey's offer will take care of my future very nicely. I regret the adverse effect this may have on each of your concerns. Mr. Grey is here to work out the final details of the deal, which is why my attorney, Mr. Barten, is also here. I thought you all should meet Mr. Grey, since you'll be seeing a lot of him in the months to come.''

Mayor Halon spoke up first. ''What are your plans for the Lodge, Mr. Grey? I hope you don't intend to open a nightclub or something like that.''

Grey shook his head. ''No, Mr. Halon. I know

we're not in Las Vegas. People don't come to this area to party; they come to relax and to retire. I intend to develop the property as a residential area. Retirement or vacation homes, you know.''

Harvey looked disappointed. ''You don't mean you're going to tear down the Lodge?'' His voice shook.

''Yes, Mr. Ashe, I'm afraid it must go. The land is worth much more as half-acre lots with expensive houses on them.''

Sarah seemed the most distraught. ''What about the Craft Village, all our little shops?''

''I'm sorry, Mrs. Ashe,'' explained Galen. ''I wanted you to be here especially because I know how this affects you and your associates in the village. Unfortunately, as you know, the village is part of the Lodge property. Mr. Grey will be buying out your leases as well, so you won't actually be losing anything. You can relocate your shops elsewhere on the Ridge.''

''But the Craft Village has been there for so many years. Our customers come from far away just to shop here in the mountains. I would hate to have to move.''

''I know it must be hard for you all. The Lodge has been here for so long. It is the main drawing point to the town for tourists. I realize that even in town, businesses will be affected by the loss of the vacationer trade. Which is why I asked you, Mayor, and Mr. Mast to be here. I thought you should know as soon as possible. Progress and change are inevitable, even in a small town.''

Galen seemed almost smug, as if he enjoyed telling them the news. Sarah had known him to be crass before, but this attitude was foreign to her experience.

''When exactly will this occur?'' asked Jim Mast.

''Well, as I said,'' explained Galen, ''tomorrow I will be meeting with Mr. Grey and my attorney to discuss the details of the sales contract. The exact time frame will be decided then.''

''I would like to get demolition and land clearing under way as soon as possible in the spring,'' said Grey, ''so I would anticipate a rapid closing. I'm prepared to do whatever is necessary to close this deal. Marketing studies in this region indicate that explosive residential growth is imminent.''

Everyone had again grown silent, in shock over the news. The last few bites of the meal went very quietly. Jessica stood up solemnly.

''Coffee and dessert will be served by the fireplace in the main dining room if you'd like to be seated in there,'' said Jessica with a forced smile. ''We have prepared a marvelous marble cheesecake and lemon pie.''

Jessica disappeared into the main dining room, as everyone else began to get up from the table. Casual conversation had resumed, though somewhat subdued. Harvey could hear the grandfather clock chiming the hour in the lobby as Jessica came out of the business office.

"Miss Roma," Jessica called, "there is a phone call for you."

Helen looked puzzled as she moved toward the office.

"Who could that be," Helen asked, "calling me here at this time of the evening?"

"I don't know," said Jessica. "She didn't identify herself."

"Very well, I'll take it in John's office," she said, walking in that direction.

Hearing this, Harvey suddenly remembered a task.

"That reminds me," said Harvey to Jessica. "I was supposed to call my assistant tonight to see if everything went okay in services. What phone can I use?"

"You can use the one at the front desk," she replied.

"Thank you," said Harvey as he walked into the lobby. He reached for the phone, but noticed both lines were busy, so he stood there waiting for an open line. He looked around to see Jim Mast and the mayor walking toward the lobby, mumbling to each other. They split up at the lobby, Mast going out the front door. In a moment he could see a cigarette lighter flickering against the wind under the front canopy. The mayor had gone upstairs. He also saw the brunette, whom he heard Barten call Julie, going toward the rest rooms. Scott Grey had gone into the solarium on the far side of the dining room.

He could also see Galen, Jessica, and the chef going back and forth between the kitchen and dining room, clearing off the table and setting up coffee and dessert trays by the fireplace. He then heard Jessica ask Galen to go outside and get firewood. Sarah seemed to be the only guest not doing anything, only sitting by the fireplace, trying to get warm. She looked frozen, but Harvey could tell it was more emotional than physical. He could not see if Mr. Barten had come out of the private dining room.

Harvey looked back at the phone, and the lines were still busy. Sighing, he folded his arms, trying to remain patient. He looked at his watch and realized eight minutes had passed. He glanced up to see Sarah winking at him from her seat, and blew a discreet kiss. It allowed Harvey to forget his impatience momentarily. He was glad to see Sarah looking less forlorn.

Finally, he saw one line go blank, and he immediately picked up the phone to make his call.

After talking to his assistant pastor for about ten minutes, he rejoined Sarah in the dining room. Gradually, everyone else returned to the dining room from their various errands to have dessert. Jessica began to pour coffee.

"How did the service go, Harvey?" Sarah asked, her voice no longer quivering.

"Jason said the crowd was pretty low because of

the weather. But the service was good, and he *said* he preached a great sermon.''

"Has anyone seen John?'' Helen Roma asked, sipping her coffee. "I haven't seen him since dinner.''

"He went out to get firewood,'' replied Jessica, "but that was twenty minutes ago. He should be back by now.''

With that, Helen put down her coffee and walked toward the kitchen. The door to the kitchen was open, and Harvey watched Helen walk to the back door and open it. The wind and snow whipped in around her legs. She stood there looking intently outside, trying to locate Galen. She called his name several times, but the wind was too loud for her voice to carry very far.

Then . . . she screamed. Sarah was startled in her seat by the shrill, bloodcurdling sound. Everyone else jumped up and ran to the kitchen.

"Outside!'' Helen yelled. "The woodshed . . . John's trapped . . . someone help him!''

Harvey and all the rest of the men ran outside into the storm. The air was biting, the wind in their eyes. As they went down the path, approaching the shed, they could see legs poking out from under the collapsed roof of the small shed. They tried to lift the roof, but the snow piled on top made it too heavy.

Mast picked up a shovel lying on the ground near the shed and began scraping snow off of the roof. Finally, they were able to lift the roof out of the way.

There was John Galen, faceup, with blood seeping into the snow around his head.

Harvey knelt beside him, putting his nearly frozen finger on Galen's neck. Feeling no pulse, he stood up.

"Galen's dead," Harvey pronounced.

"Oh, no," said Barten. "I can't believe it."

"The snow must have collapsed the roof," ascertained Mayor Halon.

Harvey turned the body over and saw a deep gash in the back of Galen's skull, from where the blood was no longer flowing, but oozing in the cold. Then Harvey examined the two-by-four post that had supported the roof. It lay in the snow, a deep nick near its base. A realization came to his mind, and he immediately removed his hand from the body. He wrapped his arms around himself, remembering how cold it was.

"No one touch anything," he suddenly ordered, standing up.

"What's wrong?" asked Grey, his teeth chattering.

"I know what this looks like, or what it's supposed to look like, but this was not an accident. Let's get back inside quickly, before we get frostbite. We have to call the sheriff!"

Everyone followed Harvey back into the Lodge, shouting to one another over the sound of the wind. Helen met them at the door.

"How badly is he hurt?" she demanded, almost in a frenzy.

"I'm sorry, Miss Roma," said Harvey with his best minister's voice, "but I'm afraid that John Galen is dead."

Helen looked at Harvey with disbelief.

"That can't be, not John!" she cried.

"The snow collapsed the roof on him," said Mr. Mast. "He never knew what hit him."

"I'm afraid it wasn't the roof that caused his death," corrected Harvey. "I'm sorry to dispute you."

"What *are* you talking about, Reverend?" yelled the mayor, now very agitated.

"Please, please," said Harvey, motioning them back to the dining room, "everyone calm down. Let's get back in there and sit down, and then we can call the sheriff. We can deal with this if we just don't panic."

"I'll call Sheriff Randall," said Jessica, disappearing into her office. Everyone else moved back into the dining room and sat down. Sarah moved close to her husband, touching his arm gently.

"Harvey," she whispered cautiously, "what is the matter? I haven't seen you this intense in years."

Harvey took Sarah's hand. "Dear, there has been a murder here. We're not safe until the authorities arrive."

"How can you say that?" cried Helen, overhearing Harvey's comment. "Who could want to kill John?"

"My feelings exactly," added the mayor. "It was clearly an accident, Reverend Ashe. You shouldn't upset Miss Roma—and the rest of us—by jumping to conclusions.''

''I understand how you all must feel,'' said Harvey, standing up in front of the fire, rubbing his still cold hands in the warmth. ''It does seem incredible, but I'm certain of what I saw. I have been trained to notice these things, you must realize. I was a police detective years ago, before entering the ministry.''

Jim Mast walked up to him. ''Well, just what did you see, Reverend, that the rest of us missed?''

Harvey began to pace a little as he spoke. ''The position of his body is all wrong. The wound is in the back of the skull, but we found his body faceup. Anything striking him from behind with sufficient force to kill him would have caused him to fall facedown. So someone must have moved the body. Maybe they turned him over to see if he was dead; I don't know. And besides, the two-by-four post was still intact. If the weight of the snow actually caused the collapse, the post would have fractured at its weakest point. The only mark was a nick in the wood near the base. And last, the shovel that you, Mr. Mast, found lying on the snow—it had to have been dropped there just minutes earlier, otherwise it would have been buried in the snow.''

The room was deathly quiet, except for the crackling of the fire. The reality of their situation was now sinking in. Worried glances played on their faces.

''So just what are you implying?'' asked Barten.

His voice suggested he knew what Harvey was leading to, but didn't want to believe it.

Harvey sat down again by Sarah.

"It's obvious," he concluded, "someone has killed John Galen with a blow to the back of the skull, and tried to make it look like an accident, sloppily and hastily, I might add. It was apparently not thought out ahead of time. Someone saw an opportunity and rashly carried it out."

"So you mean someone is out there, stalking us?" asked Helen. "Like in some cheap horror movie, waiting for a chance to kill each one of us?" Hysteria sharpened her voice and her gray eyes were wide open.

"No, Miss Roma," said Harvey, "I don't think anyone is outside. No one could survive very long out there. We're miles from any house or place of business; the roads are closed. It must be someone here, in the Lodge."

Mistrusting looks were exchanged as each one looked with accusing eyes at who they thought was the most suspicious.

"What do we do now?" asked the mayor.

"We have no choice but to wait for the sheriff."

Jessica Barrow had just entered the room. "It will be a long wait, Reverend."

"Why?" he asked.

"Sheriff Randall says that the blizzard has worsened. The road to the Lodge is impassable, even to his four-wheel drive with snow chains. He's calling in equipment from the next county to help plow the snow, but he doesn't think he can get here until sometime tomorrow. We're on our own tonight.''

''It is my recommendation, then,'' said Harvey, ''that we all retire for the night, and stay securely locked in our rooms until Sheriff Randall can get here. In the meantime I suggest that we mark where Mr. Galen's body is before the snow gets any deeper. Miss Barrow, is there something we can use to surround the area until the police arrive?''

Jessica thought for a moment. ''Yes, as a matter of fact there is a grounds keeper's shed with tools and gardening stuff, like pickets and snow fencing. Could you use that?''

''Yes,'' Harvey said, ''I think that will do. Also, is there a camera in the lodge?''

''There's one in John's office.''

''Good, may I use it please? A photograph of the crime scene before the snow accumulates will be necessary.''

Jessica nodded and went in the side door of Galen's office, coming out in a moment with a Polaroid camera.

''One last thing,'' Harvey said before the group split up. ''No one should be alone. We all should move about in threes.''

''Why threes?'' asked Mast.

Harvey stood face-to-face with Mast. "If I'm the killer, would you want to be alone with me?"

Mast nodded without a word, and joined Barten and the mayor in going out to mark the site of the murder of the late Mr. Galen.

In a few minutes Harvey had returned to the dining room with pictures in hand. The mayor and Jim Mast followed him. Harvey was feverishly studying the various shots he'd made with the camera when he looked up to see Sarah sitting next to Helen Roma on the couch. She was gently holding her hand, and speaking softly to her. He couldn't discern the words, but he knew they would be words of comfort. Helen was quiet, staring blankly into the flames. She had hardly spoken. Harvey began to realize his own callousness. In the heat of the moment, he had become engaged in the crime at hand, reverting to his old self, the tough police detective.

Then he remembered his true duty, in accordance with his calling and life's work. He felt compassion for the grieving Helen Roma. In the excitement she was almost forgotten.

"Miss Roma," said Harvey gently as he sat on the hearth beside the couch, "I am deeply sorry for what has happened. I know that at such times understanding doesn't come easy. I realize that this is not the time or place, but if later, tomorrow perhaps, you would like to talk, perhaps I can offer some words of encouragement.''

Helen smiled politely, but just barely. ''Thank you, Reverend. Perhaps I'll take you up on that. It's just so much of a shock. I can't imagine what purpose anyone would have in . . .'' Her voice began to break and her reddened eyes shut tightly, forcing out a tear.

''. . . I'm sorry, I . . . need to go upstairs now, if you don't mind.''

''Of course,'' Harvey said. ''We'll talk tomorrow. You'll need your strength, because, you see, the police will determine the purpose in this. The questioning is not easy, so please rest.''

A cloud of steam rolled out of the bathroom as Harvey opened the door, tying the cords of his velour robe. The hot shower had relaxed his tense body, but his mind refused to erase the image of the gash in John Galen's skull. Years ago, death was a daily thing for Harvey. His old job had desensitized him toward even the most ghastly of murders. Somehow, this was different. It had been many years since he had faced a corpse outside of a funeral service. Even in his years as a police detective, he had never investigated the murder of someone he'd actually known. They were all strangers, and might as well have been mannequins. John Galen's blood seeping into the snow was an unnerving sight for him.

He turned off the bathroom light, and saw Sarah sitting on the side of the bed. Her gentle features were beautiful in the soft light of the bedside lamp. However, her expression was one of worry and fear.

Harvey moved to her side and slid his muscular arm around her shoulder.

"I wish that you hadn't had to face this, dear," he said softly. "I know John was a friend of yours."

"It isn't just that, Harvey," she said, smoothing the wrinkles in her nightgown. "I didn't really know John all that well, just a casual business acquaintance, you know. But to see him dead like that. I've never been around a death like this, where someone was . . . murdered."

"It's been a long time for me, too, Sarah, but we'll get through this. We always do, don't we?"

"I know." Sarah placed her hand on Harvey's. "I just wish we had stayed home. We could be sitting beside our own fireplace right now, drinking hot chocolate, and just being together."

"And petting the cats?"

Sarah laughed. "Yes, and petting your babies. But instead, we're trapped here, with all this going on."

Harvey didn't speak, knowing she was right. Instead, he held her close, so at least she would know that he was there, and would protect her.

". . . yes, I know he needs to speak to you . . ." said a frantic Janice Crumb into the phone, "Hold one moment!"

The sheriff's small office had become bedlam. It

was usually a very quiet place, but now the phone was ringing constantly. Janice had hoped she would be able to get home before the storm got worse, but now she realized she was there to stay. No one was going anywhere.

"Sheriff Randall!" Janice called from her desk into the office behind her. "Chief Wyatt on the phone . . ."

Jeff Randall had not seen anything like this in his brief career of public service. The blizzard had shut down the entire county. Yet instead of giving him a quiet night off, every conceivable emergency picked this night to happen. He had already had to brave the elements earlier that evening to break up a domestic fight on a farm just outside of town. On the way back he had to stop and transport Jewell Harrison to the hospital as she picked tonight to give birth to her seventh baby. He had to do this because the town's single ambulance was attending an automobile accident on the other side of the county. Townspeople were calling him to complain about losing power, as if he had anything to do with it, or could do anything about it.

Now, to add to the joy of this night, he received a call from the Briar Ridge Lodge reporting a murder.

"Mrs. Evans, I know this is hard on you, but the power trucks are having a difficult time getting by on the roads. I'm sure they'll have your power on as soon as they can . . . I know you can't watch your favorite TV show; neither can I . . . ma'am, I understand, but we're doing the best we can . . . now, Mrs. Evans, I have to go, I have a very important call coming in . . . yes . . . good night.''

Randall took a deep breath as he hung up the phone. ''Janice, put the chief through.''

In a moment, Randall's phone chirped, signaling the transferred call. He picked up the phone, pacing around the desk as he talked.

''Chief . . . yes, it's awful . . . look, have you got anything that can get me up to the Lodge? . . . I know, but you see there's been a fatality up there . . . I need to be there; it may be a murder . . . okay . . . please let me know ASAP . . . all right, 'bye.''

Randall hung up the phone with exasperation. He looked up as he heard the front door open, allowing a rush of cold air to blow into his office. It was Laura and Timothy Pace, barely recognizable under their winter wrappings.

''Laura, what are you doing here?'' said Janice.

Randall came quickly out of his office. ''Timothy, Laura, you should be at home. This is no place for you!''

''Mom and Dad are up on that mountain, I'm worried, and our phone is out!''

''I know, Laura, a lot of things are out tonight.''

''Have you heard from them?'' asked Timothy.

Randall hesitated. ''Yes, I talked to Jessica Barrow, the assistant manager. Harvey and Sarah are all right, but we lost the phone connection before I could speak with your father.''

Laura could sense the apprehension in the sheriff's voice.

''Something's happened, hasn't it?'' she surmised.

''Laura, your parents are fine, but there has been . . . an accident. It involved John Galen, the owner. Unfortunately, he didn't survive.''

''What kind of accident?'' demanded Timothy. ''Is there any danger for the others?''

Randall looked down at the floor, then looked up and motioned to his office. ''Maybe we should talk in here . . .''

''No, Sheriff,'' said Laura, now clearly worried. ''Tell us what is going on. We have the right to know. Are my parents in any danger?''

Randall was now massaging his throbbing head. ''Laura, we think John Galen may have been murdered.''

''Oh, no,'' said Timothy. ''Are you going up there?''

''I've been trying, but the weather has prevented us from getting up the mountain.''

''Then *I'll* try. My four-wheel-drive truck will make it.''

''No, Timothy! I can't let you go up that mountain tonight! Your truck may get you around town, but the road to the Lodge is impassable. You'll get stuck out there, and I doubt anyone could survive for long in this blizzard. There's nothing you can do.''

''Well, what *are* you doing?'' said Laura, almost in tears.

''I'm trying to get help from other counties. Creek County has some bigger equipment that might help, but their hands are full, too. Trust me, Harvey is my friend. I'm doing everything I can. Now you two get home before you get stranded here yourself. Consider that an order.''

Timothy took Laura in his arms. ''Come on, honey, there's nothing we can do.''

Laura wiped a worried tear from her eyes. ''Yes, there is, Timothy. We can pray for them, all night if we have to.''

Timothy nodded as he led her back out to the truck.

''Sheriff . . .'' called Janice, ''Joe Snyder is on the phone. He said someone's broken in his store and looted it!''

''Oh, just great.'' The sheriff moaned. ''Will this night never end?''

Chapter Two

A dingy grayness glowing through the window signaled that morning had come. An angry wind still whistled under the eaves of the lodge as Harvey awoke from a light and troubled sleep. He reached his arm across to Sarah, but she wasn't in the bed. Harvey sat up and saw Sarah sitting in a chair by the large picture window, watching the snow continue.

The room seemed cold and Harvey wondered if the heat was working. He put on his robe and walked over to Sarah.

"Are you still worried, Sarah?" Harvey asked, putting his large hand to her back. "Did you sleep at all?"

"A little," she said simply. "I feel very cut off and

helpless. Harvey, are you quite sure that this whole thing wasn't just a freak accident?''

Harvey sat down next to his wife. ''Yes, dear, I'm quite certain.''

''Then we are in danger until the police arrive, until we can leave and go home?''

''I won't lie to you, Sarah. There is danger where there is murder. But I won't let anything happen to you . . . on my life!''

Sarah nodded, taking his hand. ''I'd never doubt your devotion, or your prowess. But here, miles from town, isolated . . . you can't exactly call for backup like you did in the old days. I can't help it, I still worry.''

''I know, Sarah, so do I.''

There was a knock at the door, gentle at first, but then more forceful. Harvey took on a look of suspicion—then readiness. He went to the dresser, and reached into a pocket inside his open suitcase. He produced a small pistol, and discreetly placed it into the pocket of his robe. Sarah had often complained to Harvey about carrying the pistol when they traveled, or even having it in the house. She didn't think it was appropriate for a pastor; it seemed so mistrusting. Harvey had been a police detective for too many years, however, to have it any other way. He had seen too much in his years on the force. He was very sure of human nature, and knew how deceiving outward appearances were. He also knew that nothing in his religious training contradicted this conclusion. If anything, it completely reinforced his caution.

Harvey went over to the door, where someone was still knocking persistently.

"Who is it?" Harvey called through the door.

"Jessica Barrow," came the muffled voice.

"Miss Barrow, in the interest of safety, I thought we had agreed to stay locked in our rooms until the police arrive."

"I need to talk to you, Mr. Ashe. It's very important. May I please come in?"

"Harvey," said Sarah, "I think you should let her in."

"Just a minute, honey," he retorted. Harvey moved closer to the door. "Are you alone, Miss Barrow?"

"Yes, Reverend."

Harvey reached up and turned the latch with his left hand, keeping the right one firmly grasped on the pistol in his robe pocket. The door opened, and Jessica Barrow stood there, white with fright.

"Come in, Miss Barrow."

Looking both ways down the hall first, Jessica came inside, closing and locking the door behind her. Harvey had backed up to the other side of the room, not allowing her to get too close.

"I'm sorry to seem so mistrusting, Miss Barrow, but until help arrives, the less contact between those here, the better."

"That's just it, Reverend," she began. "The police

aren't coming, at least not today. Maybe not tomorrow. The storm has gotten worse. Travel is impossible. Sheriff Randall called early this morning to say he can't get here. Now the phone lines are down. The ice has snapped the lines. Only the generator is keeping the power on here at the Lodge. So, you see, we're totally alone.''

"Oh, this is just awful," said Sarah.

"The situation is grave, I'll agree," said Harvey. "What do you want me to do?"

"Reverend, I've been told you were once a police detective in the city, years ago. I know that it's an imposition; I know that it is asking you to perhaps endanger your own life. But I ask you anyway. Will you take charge of this matter until the police arrive?"

"In what way? I'm no bodyguard, just a middle-aged country preacher."

"No, Reverend. I'm not asking for protection. I'm asking you to find out who it was, to investigate and reveal the killer. If you can figure it out and at least confine the responsible person, the rest of us can sleep a little easier until help arrives."

"Oh, no, Miss Barrow. That's not my place. I haven't done police work in years. It would not be appropriate for me to question the guests. I have no authority."

"Yes, you do. During our last conversation, Sheriff Randall informed me that two years ago he deputized you during a search for a lost child. That title is still valid. You do represent the law here, and you *must* do it for our safety. As well as your own.''

Harvey sat down in the chair again, in deep thought. She was right, of course. He was still legally a deputy, and the danger to the guests was very real. He wondered if this was the right thing to do, morally and ethically.

''Reverend,'' Jessica prompted, ''what do you say?''

Harvey remained in silent thought.

''Harvey,'' said Sarah, ''you must do what's right; don't let fear for me cloud the decision. I will stand beside you whatever happens, as I always have.''

Before Harvey could speak, there came another knock at the door, this one sounding frantic.

''We've become popular this morning,'' said Harvey. He walked over to the door, still clutching the pistol in his pocket.

''Who is it?'' he called through the door.

A muffled but worried voice came through the door. ''It's Floyd. Is Miss Barrow there?''

Jessica said, ''It's Floyd Helton, my chef. I told him I'd be speaking with you.''

''Why isn't he in *his* room?'' asked Harvey.

''He insisted on cooking breakfast. He's just that way; no murder can stop him from doing his job. And after all, we must eat, you know.''

Harvey nodded, as Helton continued to knock. He

turned the latch and opened the door. Helton was wringing his hands nervously.

"What is it, Floyd?" asked Jessica.

"It's Lisa," came the explanation worriedly. "I needed to start breakfast. She said last night that she would help set the tables and set up the buffet. When she didn't show, I called her room. She didn't answer. I'm worried!"

"Breakfast? Buffets?" said Harvey. "Am I the only one locked in my room?"

"Reverend," said Jessica, "He's working based on my instructions. We just don't have the staff to serve everyone in their rooms. As long as we all stay together, I think we'll be all right."

"I suppose you're right."

"Okay, Floyd," said Jessica, "let's go see what's keeping Lisa."

Harvey, still in his robe, followed Jessica and Helton down the hall and around the corner to Lisa Aames's room. It was, of course, still locked. Jessica knocked, rather forcefully. There was no answer.

"Lisa!" she called through the door. "It's Jessica. Are you in there?"

Still there was no answer. Jessica reached in her skirt pocket, retrieving a key ring. She placed the pass-key in the door lock and opened it. Harvey stood directly behind her, looking over his shoulder.

The room was dark, but a sliver of light sliced

across the room from the partially open bathroom door. Jessica flicked on the light as she moved inside.

''Lisa,'' she called.

''The bathroom.'' Harvey pointed.

Jessica nodded and pushed the door, which was slightly ajar. Lisa was not there, but the counter was a shambles. Her overnight bag was open and on its side. Most of the contents were strewn on the counter, in the sink, or on the floor. Clearly someone had been desperately searching for something.

''Lisa!'' cried Floyd as he saw a pair of legs on the floor beyond the bed. Immediately, he rushed to her side. Harvey, Sarah, and Jessica were soon behind him.

Lisa Aames was sprawled on the floor as if she had fainted. Beside her right hand lay a small gray device, about the size of a calculator. On the nightstand was a box of small plastic strips, torn open with apparent desperation. Harvey also noticed what looked like a pen on the floor, half beneath the bed. He immediately checked Lisa's pulse. He shook his head dourly.

''I'm very sorry,'' Harvey reported as he stood, ''but she's dead. I'd say for several hours at least.''

''I wonder what this thing is?'' said Harvey, gesturing toward the gray device. ''Don't anybody touch or disturb anything. Remember, this could be a crime scene, too.''

''I think that's her blood sugar tester, Reverend,'' explained Floyd. ''She's diabetic, you know.''

"No, I didn't know."

Harvey gingerly pushed the single button on the top of the device, his finger wrapped in a tissue he'd gotten from the bathroom. The LCD screen lit up, displaying a single number.

"622," mumbled Harvey.

"But what happened?" said Floyd, still shocked.

"I'm no doctor. We'll have to wait for a professional opinion to be sure. But this much is obvious. As a diabetic, she was in some kind of physical distress, and trying to take her blood sugar reading when she passed out. I don't know enough about diabetes to know what that number means. I'd imagine it wasn't good news for her. Jessica, did you know much about her medical condition?"

Jessica had tried not to look at Lisa's body, especially her face. Instead, she had been staring at the flowers on the bedspread. Harvey's question caused her to gaze at the blank and confused expression that death had frozen onto Lisa's face.

"I didn't pry too much into her personal affairs, Reverend," she explained, "but I know she had trouble with her illness from time to time. She had been out sick frequently, and even had to go to the hospital a couple of times. I don't think she controlled her diabetes very well."

Sarah flicked on the light above the nightstand. A package of syringes was opened and half empty. On the floor was a bottle of insulin. The used syringe was on the floor next to the trash can.

"It seems she tried to take her insulin," said Sarah, turning their attention to her discovery, "but it was too little too late, I suppose."

Harvey came around the bed and knelt where the items had fallen. He peered closely at the insulin bottle. From what he could see, only a few drops remained in the bottom.

"Maybe she had run out," theorized Sarah.

Harvey stared intently at the used syringe. "There's residue of liquid in the syringe. She had enough for one dose at least."

"Surely, she would have extra."

Jessica turned away from the body toward Harvey. "Lisa sometimes kept extra in the refrigerator downstairs. But if she was in bad shape, maybe she couldn't make it down there."

Harvey stood up, hands on his hips. "Did she seem all right to you yesterday?"

Jessica scratched her head as she thought. "I only noticed she seemed incessantly thirsty. I think she had a big glass of water most of her shift. That was unusual for her, but I thought she had started some new diet or something. She also didn't seem to be able to concentrate on her work, but she was often like that anyway. Young girls often are when they don't take their jobs seriously."

"I remember she didn't look well at all when we

arrived last night," remembered Sarah. "She looked very sickly to me, and her hands were shaking. This must have been building up for some time."

Floyd had stood up from Lisa's crumpled body, with a single tear in his eye.

"Lisa had a lot of maturing to do, Jessica, but she did take her job seriously, despite what you think."

"I'm sorry, Floyd, I didn't mean to sound critical of her. I know she was very dear to you. I just meant that her frivolity did not strike me as odd at the time. But now, I suppose, perhaps she was not feeling well."

Harvey sighed, looking perplexed.

"Not being a doctor, I'm certainly no expert on diabetes. But it's hard to imagine someone dying that quickly from missing a single dose of insulin. I think it takes more to cause death."

"What's your point, Reverend?" asked Jessica.

"I'm not sure if I have a point, Jessica. But one thing I do know, I'm going to take you up on your request."

"My request?"

"To investigate this matter, to find the killer responsible for John Galen's death."

"Why the sudden change in heart?"

"I don't know, Jessica, I just have a very bad feeling about all this. It just doesn't seem right to me. I want to get to the bottom of it. It bugs me, and I don't like to be bugged."

Sarah sat next to Harvey, putting her hand on his knee. "You think Lisa's death is related to John's?"

"I think we'd be jumping to conclusions to say that right now, dear. But in our situation, shut off from the rest of the world, locked in with an unknown killer, I can't take the chance."

Harvey stood up and Sarah followed. His usually pleasant expression was now grim, or even angry.

" 'Cursed be he that smiteth his neighbor secretly . . . ' " said Harvey quietly, almost to himself, but with indignation.

"What was that, Reverend?" said Jessica. "I didn't quite hear you."

"Just a quotation, from the ultimate police manual."

"Oh."

"Now, give me a few minutes to get cleaned up and dressed. Jessica, is there a discreet location, inaccessible and lockable, where we can keep Miss Aames's body until the police arrive? As much as I hate to disturb the scene, we don't want the body to start to deteriorate."

"There's a walk-in refrigerator unit in the convention hall. It has a padlock. Would that be okay?" Jessica asked.

"That will be fine. Floyd, help me take the body there. Jessica, I'll need that camera again. And please assemble last night's meeting participants in the dining room. Lock Miss Aames's room. I'll see you downstairs.''

"As you say, Reverend," said Jessica, as Harvey leaned over the body and Sarah rushed out into the hall toward their room. Jessica felt Floyd's hand rest gently on her shoulder.

"Don't worry, Jessica," said Floyd in a reassuring tone, "it will all be over soon."

"I just hope I'm doing the right thing by getting the Reverend involved in this."

"I know that you've made the best decision you possibly can. I feel better just knowing he's in charge."

Jessica patted the hand resting on her shoulder, and displayed a forced smile before proceeding down the hall.

Harvey was sitting on the end of the bed, tying his shoe. This task was not as easy as it once was in his younger, slimmer years. He groaned as he straightened up. Sarah pretended not to notice.

"Why are you so suspicious about Lisa all of a sudden?" asked Sarah as she tucked in her blouse. "I know it's awful what's happened to her, but you really think she's been murdered, too, don't you?"

Harvey stood up, reaching for the room key on the dresser.

"I keep thinking about that conversation I partially overheard last night."

''You mean on the stairs, before dinner?''

''Yes.''

''Well, who was she talking to?''

''That's just it, I don't know. By the time we got down there, whoever it was had left the room. But I remember one thing. Lisa distinctly said, 'Eight o'clock, yes, I'll remember' . . . or something like that.''

''Wasn't it just after eight when we discovered John Galen's body?''

''My point exactly. And on top of that, she was the *only* one here who did not come to the dinner. In fact, she was forgotten during the whole thing.''

''You think she knew something?''

''Maybe, but it's too early to tell. Are you ready? We need to get down there.'' Sarah nodded, and followed Harvey into the hall.

All who had been present at the time of John Galen's murder had gathered according to Harvey Ashe's request.

Seated on the ornate lounger before the fireplace were Helen Roma, Benjamin Barten, and his girlfriend Julie Gilreath. Mayor Halon stood by the fireplace, leaning on the mantel, drinking coffee. Jim Mast sat in a velour high-backed chair, next to the fireplace. He looked like a king sitting on his throne. Scott Grey, who would have owned the Briar Ridge Lodge that day, paced nervously behind the couch. Floyd Helton sat at a table close by, toying with the salt shaker as he waited.

Harvey and Sarah were just coming into the dining room as Jessica Barrow explained the situation. She was standing in front of the fireplace as she spoke.

". . . and therefore, on Sheriff Randall's authority and recommendation, we have asked Reverend Ashe to investigate this murder. We are expected to answer his questions, and for our own safety, to follow his instructions. Until the storm lets up and the police arrive, he is in charge. Are there any questions or objections?"

"Sure, why not?" Jim Mast laughed. "Let Sherlock have his fun."

"Jim!" scolded Mayor Halon. "This is not a humorous matter."

"You're right, it's not," retorted Mast. "Which is why I can't believe you'd allow this, Robert. You're the mayor of this town. You should be the authority here—not some preacher trying to get publicity."

"I suppose you'd be more qualified to investigate a murder?" replied Halon. "I'm not a detective, Jim, and neither are you. I'm just a small-town businessman. I gladly concede to his wisdom and experience. Why, I remember reading years ago about how he solved this serial murder case in the city where—"

Harvey Ashe stopped the mayor's dissertation, putting his hand on Halon's shoulder.

"Please, Mayor," Harvey interrupted, "let's not be-labor my résumé. Mr. Mast, I don't want to do this either. Initially, I declined to do it. I felt it was best that we waited for the police. But then, after what we found this morning . . . what happened to Miss Aames . . .''

''What?'' demanded Barten. ''Who's Miss Aames?''

''Lisa was the desk clerk who checked you in yesterday. She wasn't even down here with us last night. Yet this morning she was found dead in her room. It appeared to be related to her condition as a diabetic. But for some reason, I have doubts about it. In either case, a murderer is still among us. We are all in danger. Let's work together for our own safety, before another one dies. No one is coming to help us. We are alone, and vulnerable. We must act. Are you all with me? If not, Sarah and I will lock ourselves in our room and you all can fend for yourselves. What will it be?''

The room was silent, except for the crackle of the fire and the wind blowing snow against the windows.

''Well, what do you want us to do?'' asked a still-belligerent Jim Mast.

''Last night's rules remain in effect,'' announced Harvey. ''We need to stay in large groups, no fewer than three. No one goes anywhere alone. Miss Barrow, I will need a room where I can talk to each one, privately.''

''You can use John's office,'' replied Jessica.

''That will be excellent. We'll start immediately.''

Harvey turned back toward the group. ''I know some of you are frightened, some are angry. I feel the same way. But if we stick together, we'll get through this.''

Jessica motioned toward John Galen's office. Harvey and Sarah followed her. Once inside, Harvey closed the door, and immediately began looking around the room.

Like the Lodge, the office was old and rustic. The walls were lined with a dark paneling, and with only one window, the room seemed dark even with the light on. The desk was a grand old maple construction. The top was strewn with papers, documents, notes, and bills such that Harvey could barely see the wood. The slick new PC seemed strangely out of place sitting on the antique desk. There were a couple of leather-back chairs against the wall in front of him, and behind the desk, some shelves mounted on the wall displayed trinkets, trophies, and other clutter that must have meant much to John Galen. He had entered the office from the door leading to the lobby, but now Harvey saw another door on the other side of the office. It was open, and Harvey got up and went to it. It led to the kitchen, and across the kitchen, he could clearly see the back door leading to the woodshed where Galen had ended his career.

To his left he could see the refrigerator. His curiosity aroused, he went to it and looked inside. It was filled with all the things one would expect a commer-

cial kitchen's refrigerator to contain. On the top shelf
Harvey saw a blue insulated lunch carrier. The name
LISA was written in black marker on the side. Sarah
had walked over next to him as he used a pencil to
pull it out of the refrigerator and open it. It contained
the usual assortment of lunch items. There was a tur-
key sandwich, a bag of potato chips, and some
cookies.

''Double chocolate chip,'' remarked Harvey. ''Not
the best choice for an insulin-dependent diabetic,
wouldn't you say?''

Sarah nodded. Then Harvey used the pencil to fish
out a plastic bag containing medicine bottles. He could
see their labels through the plastic bag.

''Extra insulin,'' Sarah noted.

''Yes . . . and what's this?'' Harvey said, looking at
another bottle. ''Glucagon? Any idea what that's
for?''

''Not a clue, Harvey. I've never known anyone with
diabetes.''

''Well, I'll hang on to this all the same. It may be
important to the medical examiner.''

Harvey stuffed the plastic bag in his pocket. He replaced the lunch carrier and closed the refrigerator
door.

Harvey then walked back toward the office, taking
one more general look, noticing the layer of dust covering everything except the desk surface where John
worked. The office was definitely homey, but much

too disorganized for Harvey. He knew he could never function here for long.

"Jessica," began Harvey as he moved back to the desk, "are there any plans of the Lodge?"

Jessica turned toward the last filing cabinet, the lower drawer.

"Yes, I think John kept them in here," she said. She pulled open the squeaky drawer with some difficulty, and produced the rolled-up blueprints of the Lodge. They were yellow with age, and as Harvey unrolled them they made a crackling sound. Harvey hoped that they wouldn't disintegrate in his hands. He could see there were several pages, and he flipped to the page showing the main floor with the dining rooms, kitchen, and lobby area. The rest of the plans he rolled back up and placed next to the desk. He laid the drawing on the desk, pushing the papers out of the way, but the old scroll kept rolling back up in protest.

"Sarah, can you hand me something I can hold these edges down with?" said Harvey as he struggled with the uncooperative paper.

Sarah reached up to the dust-covered shelf behind the desk and retrieved a few likely paperweights, adding to the marks in the dust. The plans successfully secured, Harvey began to study them, stroking his mustache. After a few moments, Harvey opened the lap drawer of the desk, and began rummaging through the clutter.

''What are you looking for, Reverend?'' ask Jessica, trying to help.

''Some of those little yellow note stickers. Do you have any?''

''Look in the right-hand junk drawer,'' Jessica replied.

''It appears that all the drawers match that description,'' commented Harvey. At last, he found the pad of note stickers, handing them to his wife.

''Sarah, if you will please put everyone's name on one label each, we can keep up with the movements as they give their side of the story.''

Jessica walked toward the lobby door as Sarah started writing names artistically on the note stickers.

''Who do you want to question first, Reverend?'' asked Jessica as she reached for the door.

''Why . . . you, Miss Jessica Barrow!''

Chapter Three

Jessica was surprised as she discreetly closed the door. She turned and looked at Harvey with a sudden reluctance. She sat down in the chair before the large desk where Harvey had taken his seat.

"Okay, Reverend Ashe," she said quietly, propping her elbow on the arm of the chair, "what do you want to know?"

"Jessica," Harvey said, leaning over the desk, "surely you didn't think I'd leave you out of this, did you?"

"I guess I thought we'd just work together. You know, I didn't count on being a suspect."

Jessica looked straight at Harvey with piercing eyes, as if daring him to say what he really thought. Sarah stood silently beside Harvey, suddenly nervous at the tension caused by Jessica's demeanor.

"I didn't say you were a suspect, Miss Barrow," Harvey stated calmly and deliberately, "but after all, you stand to be out of a job if the Lodge is torn down . . . right?"

"Certainly. But I wouldn't kill for that. There are other hotels, and other jobs. Besides, why would I urge you to work on the case if I myself were the killer?"

"What better way to deflect suspicion than to start the investigation yourself, and to make sure someone who is *not* a professional is in charge? Rather increases the chances for success, don't you think?"

Jessica sighed, and sat up straight in her chair. "I suppose you're right, Reverend. I don't mean to be a troublemaker in your first interrogation."

Harvey relaxed in the chair. It squeaked as he leaned back.

"Well, perhaps you shouldn't assume my wanting your version of the events and some background information constitutes an accusation, or suspicion on my part."

Jessica nodded, and seemed to relax at Harvey's reassurance. Sarah finally let out the breath she had been holding, and also took a seat next to Harvey.

Harvey reached into his pocket and produced the hand-held recorder he often used to make sermon notes. He set it on the desk on top of the blueprints.

"You don't mind if I keep a record of our conversation, do you?" he asked.

Jessica shook her head, and motioned for him to continue. Harvey pushed the record button on the machine. Its motor made a gentle whirring noise as the tape rolled across the recording heads.

"Miss Barrow," Harvey began softly, "since my wife and I moved here a couple of years ago, I haven't really gotten to know a lot of the people here outside our church family. Can you tell me a little bit about yourself?"

"What do you want to know?"

"Where are you from? And what brought you to Laurel Springs, and the Lodge?"

Jessica looked off to one side, as if looking into the past. "John and I go—went—way back. We're both from Philadelphia. Our families have been friends for a long time. I guess I looked up to John like an uncle, or a big brother. My parents weren't able to put me through college . . . John made sure I went, you know, made sure the money was there."

"John was very well off, then, would you say?"

"I don't guess he was really rich, but he had a large inheritance from his parents, and well, he never lacked for anything he really needed or wanted. When he decided to buy this place, he gave me the chance to work with him. He thought it would be good experience for my future career. You know, give me a good entry on my résumé to go along with my management degree."

"He seemed to really take an interest in you, didn't he?"

"Yes, well, we were very close. Like I said, he was like an uncle to me."

Jessica reached into her pocket, producing a tissue which she used to wipe her moist eyes.

"That's why it's so important to me that you expose this murderer," she continued. "Whoever it is must be brought to justice."

"I understand, Jessica," said Harvey with a warm confidence coming from years of pastoral counseling. "I know this is difficult. In this life, we are constantly faced with storms, trials, and heartbreaks. It is how we deal with them that strengthens character and spiritual maturity."

Jessica smiled thinly. "I know, Reverend, but they still hurt, don't they?"

"Yes, they do."

Jessica leaned forward, clasping her hands together to keep them from shaking.

"I'll be all right," she said. "Let's get on with this."

Harvey nodded, and moved the recorder to one side, again smoothing out the aging drawings.

"Jessica, please show me exactly where you were when Mr. Galen was . . . attacked."

Jessica pulled the chair closer to the desk so she could see, and began to study the schematic.

"Floyd and I were rushing back and forth between

the dining room and the kitchen, trying to clear off the supper dishes. There was approximately a twenty-minute period that's in question. I could have been anywhere in this area at that exact moment.''

''So you could actually have been in the kitchen when it happened?''

Jessica's brow furrowed in doubt. ''I don't think so. How could John have been killed while I stood right there in the kitchen, only a few yards from him?''

''You said you were very busy, rushing about, probably clanging pots and pans, and so forth. With the noise of the wind outside, and the poor visibility, I doubt you would have noticed anything at that moment.''

''That's true; things were very hectic at that time. And everybody else was scattered all over the place. Anyone could have done it.''

''But more than likely, only one did. Who did you see in the kitchen during that time?''

Jessica thought for a moment, trying to reconstruct her memories. ''I can definitely remember only Floyd. Except for John, of course, when he went out to get the wood. But there were times I was nowhere near the kitchen.''

''I realize that. Do you have any recollection of where any of the others were?''

Jessica shook her head confidently, and sat back in her chair. ''No, I was too busy to notice anything else.''

"You mean you didn't notice me looking out the back window at the storm?"

Jessica suddenly looked confused. "Reverend, you were using the phone during that time, in the lobby. You never stood over by the back windows."

Harvey smiled. "Still not so sure of your memory, Jessica?"

Jessica laughed softly, with embarrassment. "Did they teach you that little trick in seminary?"

"Just something I picked up along the way."

"Your point is taken, Reverend, but honestly, it's such a jumble, I need a little time to sort it out, you know."

"Certainly," Harvey agreed. "Oh, I did want to ask you one last thing, Jessica. Being assistant manager, you do have a set of master keys to all the rooms, right?"

"We have always kept master keys locked in a cabinet behind the front desk, of course," answered Jessica, somewhat defensively.

"Did you have a set with you last night?"

"Not when I went to bed."

"But you had them with you this morning?"

"Yes, I had already come downstairs by that time. Reverend, what is your point?"

"I have no point as of yet. I'm just sorting out facts, okay?"

Jessica nodded reluctantly.

"Who else might have access to that locked cabinet containing the master keys?"

Jessica looked upward as she thought.

"Other than myself and John, Lisa, of course. Floyd knew where they were. The full-time staff knows, but naturally, none of them are here now. I doubt anyone else would know about it unless they'd spent a lot of time around here, watching the operation, you know, noticing where we'd put things and so forth."

Harvey nodded in acknowledgment as he motioned toward the door. "I think that's all we need to discuss just now, Jessica. Why don't you give me a little time to look around the office here and then send in the next person."

Jessica nodded as she arose from her seat. "Sure, Reverend, how much time do you need?"

"Maybe an hour or so."

"What are you looking for?"

"Just clues, Miss Barrow."

Jessica pocketed her tissue and composed herself as she moved toward the door.

"Who do you want to see next?" Jessica asked with one pale hand on the doorknob.

Harvey had stood, and placed the yellow note sticker labeled *Jessica Barrow* on the blueprints in the dining room.

"I think perhaps I'd like to talk to Scott Grey, if you don't mind."

Jessica nodded as she opened the door to the lobby. "I'll send him in an hour."

As she stepped into the open doorway, she paused silently, looking back toward Harvey.

"Is there something you need to say, Jessica?" asked Harvey in his minister's voice again.

"Just that . . ." Her voice seemed again on the verge of cracking. ". . . please, find the one. I want to see him pay, for what he did, or her."

"No one wants to see justice done more than I," assured Harvey. "Whoever it is will surely stand accountable for it, either in this life or the hereafter."

Jessica nodded and walked out into the lobby, closing the office door as she left. Harvey sat down again, in deep thought.

"Harvey," Sarah asked, "what are you thinking?"

Harvey looked into Sarah's deep-green eyes and smiled. "I'm thinking that we need to look through these files, dear. Are you ready for some first-class snooping?"

Chapter Four

As she pulled the office door closed, Jessica paused to take in a deep, relaxing breath. She then walked through the lobby toward the dining room. Most of the group were huddled close to the fire. Mr. Barten had just tossed another log on the fire from the wood box next to the hearth. Jessica noticed that the mayor and Mr. Mast sat at a table next to the door leading to the solarium. They were leaning close to each other as they talked, as if not to be overheard. She saw the mayor pour the last few drops of coffee from the carafe on the table. She knew that was her chance to hear what they were talking about.

"... But how could he ever know?" the mayor whispered.

68

Jim Mast seemed unusually tense. ''Don't you think he knows how to get access to information.''

''Out here? In the middle of a blizzard?''

''This blizzard won't last forever.''

''So what? What does it matter?''

''What does it matter?!''

The mayor had to motion for Mast to keep his voice down.

''Sorry,'' continued Mast, ''but if this comes out, what do you think they'll conclude? What would *you* conclude? Besides, what if Helton—''

Mayor Halon pointed a stern finger into Mast's face. ''He won't. I've made sure of that. Now don't worry, this will all be over and—''

Mast nudged the mayor's elbow as he noticed Jessica standing behind them with a fresh carafe of coffee.

''Heat up that coffee, Mr. Mayor?'' she said with intentional politeness. Mast looked shocked, wondering how much she had overheard. The mayor seemed unfazed by her presence.

''Yes, thank you, Miss Barrow,'' said the mayor with a small-town politician's smile. ''Another pot would be great.''

Halon turned without missing a beat and resumed his talk with Mast. ''. . . now, as I was saying, we have nothing to worry about, the blizzard will be over and I'm sure we can get state funds for disaster relief. I've taken care of this town before, and I won't let anyone down this time either.''

Jessica took the empty carafe, placing it on the tray she carried. ''I'll be back to check on you gentleman later.''

Mayor Halon nodded and smiled again. The color had gone out of Mast's skin. He was visibly frightened.

''Jim,'' the mayor said, ''you have got to get a hold of yourself.''

''That nosy hotel clerk is going to be trouble. We've got to keep an eye on her.''

''She's not the problem. That preacher is.''

Harvey opened Floyd Helton's personnel file, and began flipping through the pages of useless information. A drop of coffee spilled from the cup as he took another sip, creating a brown stain on Floyd's federal withholding form. The clock indicated it had only been an hour, but Harvey felt as if he had been rummaging through old files all day. John Galen was a true paper pack rat. Everything he had ever received was jammed into one of these files. This would be great, if Harvey had any idea what to look for. He was just turning past a barely legible copy of a newspaper article about food poisoning when he heard Sarah call his name.

''Harvey,'' Sarah said, looking up from the bottom file drawer, ''this is interesting.''

"What, dear?" Harvey said as he stood up, his knees cracking as they stretched.

"This is a copy of the sales contract, when Mr. Galen bought the Lodge."

Sarah handed a folder to Harvey, who remained standing as he flipped through it. Sarah pointed to the last page of the contract, labeled *Special Stipulations and Conditions*.

"Do you see this?" she said. "This is very strange."

Harvey read the legal terminology to himself, and Sarah could see that he was trying to make sense of it in his mind.

"If I'm reading this right," he said, "the terms of this sale dictate that if John Galen dies intestate while still owning the Lodge, ownership reverts to the estate of the original owner. A man named Jordan Clarckston."

"I wonder if he's still alive?" Sarah asked.

"I don't know, but that name—Clarckston—is familiar."

"Do you think you know him?"

"No, but I've seen that name before. It stands out in my mind because of that unusual spelling."

Harvey paced around the room for a few moments thinking, then finally settled in one of the chairs facing the desk.

"Do you think this is significant, Harvey?"

"It could be. It means that if anyone here is related

to Jordan Clarckston, they have an interest in seeing this Lodge not change hands.''

Sarah sat down at the immense desk; she seemed dwarfed by it. ''How do we find out if anyone here is related to him, or if he's even alive?''

''Ordinarily it would be as easy as a few phone calls to check some county records. But isolated, here in this snowstorm, no phones, no access to the outside world, there's little we can do. We'll have to work with what we've got. One thing we haven't yet discussed—the weapon.''

''The murder weapon?''

''Of course. If we can find the weapon, the field of suspects may be narrowed. And the question of Lisa Aames still bugs me.''

''It's hard to see how it can be related.''

''I agree, but see if you can find her file, just the same.''

Sarah retrieved the first file in the personnel drawer, handing it to Harvey. He opened the folder, flipping past the payroll data sheet and tax forms.

''Lisa certainly was out sick a lot,'' noted Harvey. ''This file is full of doctor's notices and sick leave memos and copies of time cards.''

''Her diabetic condition?'' assumed Sarah.

''From these documents, it would seem so.''

''It's a pity she couldn't control her illness. I think most diabetics live normal lives if they take proper care of themselves.''

Harvey nodded. "She was either careless, or her case was very acute. Either way it's not surprising to see her die from it. Here's a memo documenting her passing out at the front desk and being taken to the emergency room."

Harvey handed the file back to Sarah.

"Does this answer your concerns about the circumstances of her death?" asked Sarah as she returned the file to its place.

"It should, but there's this gnawing feeling in the pit of my stomach that there's more to it than what it appears. I guess it's the timing of it all. And that partial conversation we heard on the stairway yesterday keeps coming back to me."

"It's still bugging you?"

"Yes. All I keep hearing in my head is Lisa saying "Eight, I won't forget." "

His sentence was interrupted by a knock at the door. Sarah got up from her chair and opened it. Scott Grey walked in, and Harvey motioned for him to sit down in the chair next to his.

"Mr. Grey, thank you for coming in. I hope you don't mind if I record our conversation for later reference." Harvey motioned toward the hand-held recorder on the desk.

"No, of course not," Grey said, although he seemed a little uneasy as he watched Sarah turn it on.

"I regret that you've been dragged into this ugly

matter,'' Harvey began. ''It seems that all your plans have been ruined by this as well.''

Grey nodded in frustrated acknowledgment. ''I can't believe I'm in the middle of all this. I just came to do a simple business transaction, and all of a sudden, I'm mixed up in some bizarre murder. We both just wanted to make a little money, you know? In fact, he acted like he'd struck it rich when I made the offer. I think he wanted to retire early anyway.''

''Then he was to make a tidy sum on this deal?''

''I made him a fair offer for the property.''

Harvey stood up, and walked over to the window, looking into the swirling patterns of windblown snow.

''Would you be offended if I asked just how much you offered Mr. Galen for the Lodge?'' asked Harvey.

''Under the circumstances, does it matter whether or not I'm offended by the question?''

Harvey smiled as he turned back toward Grey. ''I guess not. You can tell me now, or tell the police later, when they take over the case.''

''All right, Reverend Ashe, I offered him a million-five, which includes all the grounds and the Craft Village, too.''

Sarah's jaw dropped open in amazement.

''I'd say Mr. Galen could've retired comfortably on that.''

''I'd tend to agree,'' said Grey.

''This is kind of an old place, and sort of out of the way, you know. Just what brings you way out here from Las Vegas to buy property? Surely there's desirable real estate between here and there?''

''You're correct, of course, Reverend, but my family is originally from around here. Although I built my business in the west, I've always wanted to return to the Appalachians. And the real estate market for retirement homes in the mountains is quite hot these days. I think I made my motivations quite clear at last night's meeting.''

''Yes, you did. But a million-five?''

''I know that seems excessive to you, but with this location and acreage, I will still see profits in the millions when the project is done—well, I could have, had this not happened.''

''Mr. Grey, does the name Clarckston mean anything to you?''

Grey's brow was furrowed as he thought. ''Well, Clarckston is a very common name, you know. I'm sure I've known someone with it some time or another.''

''Yes, but I mean Clarckston, with a 'ck', not so common.''

''I don't think so.'' Grey seemed a little agitated at the question. ''Why do you ask? What do Clarckstons have to do with all this?''

''Maybe nothing, Mr. Grey.''

Grey shifted in his chair. ''Is there anything else, Reverend Ashe?''

Harvey returned to the desk, and picked up the yellow note sticker with Scott Grey's meticulously penned name.

"If you could just show me where you were during the incident last night . . ."

Grey stood up and looked at the blueprints, stroking his chin in thoughtful concentration.

"Well," Grey began, "for a few minutes, I was by the fire; it was dying down a little, and I was chilly. I think I threw a log on the fire, but the hotel people were running about setting up the dessert and coffee service, and I felt in the way. I went out into the solarium for a minute. We don't get much of this stuff in Las Vegas, you know. I was fascinated watching the blizzard."

Harvey put the note sticker into the solarium on the drawing.

"Did you see anything while you were out there? I mean, if you stood here at the corner"—Harvey pointed at a particular spot on the drawing—"you could just see the woodshed where Mr. Galen was killed."

Grey shook his head. "I couldn't see anything in this storm. You can't even see anything beyond a few yards even in the daytime. It was very dark."

Harvey pointed at another spot on the drawing. "I see there is another door leading from the solarium, down these stairs and onto the grounds. Did you notice if it was open?"

Grey looked at Harvey angrily. "It seemed to be

closed, but yes, I could easily have opened it and gone down the steps. But why would I? Why would I want him dead? He was about to make me a rich man . . . well, a richer man.''

''Yes, and you were going to make him rich, too. Was there maybe some reason you wanted to back out of the deal? Something you found out about the property that made you nervous?''

''Like what?'' Grey was almost shouting.

''I don't know, an encumbrance to the title? You tell me.''

''If there was, I didn't know about it. And even if I did, no papers were signed. I could legally walk away from this whole thing. I had no reason to see him dead.''

''Are you sure the name Clarckston isn't familiar?''

Grey took a deep breath to calm his nerves, and sat back down in the chair.

''I think I've told you all I can recall that's of any importance. And no, I don't know anyone named Clarckston. And I resent being questioned, even if this is officially sanctioned, without my attorney present.''

Harvey stopped his tape recorder, smiling as if greeting visitors in his church.

''Thank you, Mr. Grey, you've been most helpful.''

Grey stood to face Harvey, and spoke in a calmer voice. ''I'm sorry I got angry, Reverend. I've never been involved in anything like this before. I guess this place is closing in on me a little. I'm not used to being trapped like this.''

''I understand. Thank you again.''

Grey turned and headed out of the door, almost running into Floyd Helton.

''Lunch is in ten minutes, Reverend,'' Floyd announced. ''Do you want it in here?''

''No,'' Harvey said as he took Sarah's hand. ''We'll come out and join you. I'm a little tired of being cooped up in this office, too.''

Harvey gazed romantically into Sarah's eyes. ''Mrs. Ashe, would you care to join me for lunch? I hear they have excellent spaghetti, as messy as it gets.''

''I'd be delighted.''

Chapter Five

"Surely the murder weapon is long gone by now, Harvey," said Sarah as she sipped her iced tea. "I should think that looking for it would be a waste of time under the circumstances."

Harvey wiped spaghetti sauce from his chin with the linen napkin, finishing his bite. "I disagree, dear. The circumstances of this storm force me to conclude it's here somewhere."

Harvey spoke almost in a whisper, careful not to be overheard by those in the main dining room. Harvey and Sarah had decided to take lunch in the solarium, and it had afforded them a degree of privacy as they spoke.

"But whatever was used could have been thrown

off the side of the mountain. In this storm, under several feet of snow, it would never be found.''

''The woodshed is not that close to where the land drops off. Anyone out in that wind would be hard-pressed to even stand up straight, much less toss something that far off the side of the mountain.''

''They could have walked twenty feet to the edge.''

''We would have seen footprints in the snow. There were none, and not enough time had elapsed for them to have been filled in by fresh snow.''

Sarah rested her chin on her hand, looking out the window at the dimming of daylight.

''Yes, of course, I hadn't thought of that,'' she admitted, picking at her salad as she contemplated. ''Come to think of it, did you see footprints last night? I mean, an extra set, leading from the Lodge to the woodshed?''

Harvey shook his head in disgust. ''I'm sorry to say that by the time I realized that he had been murdered, Jim Mast and Mayor Halon and myself had already tracked up the scene pretty bad. I did look for footprints indicating an approach or retreat from some other direction. But nothing can be concluded about someone coming from the Lodge. Besides, a really sharp murderer would have walked in John's footprints to evade detection.''

''So we're back to square one, the weapon itself.''

''Exactly.''

''Well, just what are we looking for?''

''The gash in the back of Galen's head was made by a very heavy object, or a smaller one struck with greater force. Thinking about the difficulty of maneuvering something large in that wind causes me to lean toward the smaller object. The gash seemed to be from an edge of some sort.''

''Not the fabled 'blunt instrument' then?''

''No, I think perhaps some kind of tool, or implement is a more likely suspect. And I think it's here, in the Lodge, right in front of our eyes. You see, I get the impression that the murder itself was a hasty decision, brought on by the news John delivered last night. The killer had to think quickly, and grab something easy to get to, and easy to replace.''

Harvey reached for his glass, and looked up to see Jessica Barrow standing by the table, tea pitcher in hand.

''Reverend Ashe,'' she said, filling his glass, ''can I have a word with you?''

''Certainly, Miss Barrow,'' Harvey said. ''Sit down.''

Jessica pulled up a chair from an adjacent table, and looked around warily before speaking in a whisper.

''What's on your mind, Miss Barrow?'' asked Harvey.

''It's just something I think you should know. Something I overheard earlier this afternoon.''

''What?''

"Mayor Halon and Jim Mast were having breakfast. I had walked by their table to check on them."

"And what did you hear, Miss Barrow?"

"They were talking about you, Reverend."

"About Harvey?" asked an alarmed Sarah as she nervously crumbled her garlic toast. "What were they saying?"

"Well, not really about you, but they mentioned you. Oh, I'm sorry, I'm not making sense. I'm afraid this day has quite rattled me. They were talking about no one finding out about something. They were worried about you finding out. They were worried about how it might look if it got out in the open."

"What am I not to know?" asked Harvey.

"That's just it, I didn't hear that part of it. As soon as they noticed me they shut up, and the mayor started going on with some nonsense about disaster relief after the storm. They could tell I had overheard them."

Harvey placed his napkin on the table beside his plate and sat back in his chair.

"It sounds to me like you really didn't hear anything."

"Well, I know something must be going on with them. They mentioned Floyd's name, too. Jim Mast seemed terribly frightened, like if you found out, it may implicate them in the murder."

"Did you actually hear them mention the murder?"

Jessica thought for a moment before answering, "No, just that they didn't want you to know."

"I think you're jumping to conclusions, Miss Barrow, but I'll keep all this in mind. Perhaps, as we continue with the questioning, something will come to light. But all the same, keep your ears open, just in case they talk some more."

A soft whirring sound emanated from John Galen's computer as Harvey flipped the ON switch. The color monitor came to life with a bright blue background. Sarah stood behind him and watched over his shoulder.

"Harvey, do you know anything about computers? I don't want you messing up the Lodge's records."

"Dear, we have a PC at the office."

"Yes, but Corinne knows what she's doing."

"I've used it, too, you know. I'm not completely in the dark ages when it comes to technology."

"Just when it comes to selecting ties?"

Harvey allowed the last remark to pass without comment, since he couldn't really dispute it. Instead he looked at the icons that had appeared on the screen.

"I don't think we need to look into the payroll program, but here's the financial management package."

"Do you think you should look at that, Harvey? I mean, that's pretty confidential material."

"I asked Jessica a little while ago for permission. She had no problem with it."

"What do you hope to see?"

"I don't know, just anything to give us a motive,

or an indication of what was really going on in his life.''

Harvey examined the most recent transactions in the general ledger.

''Nothing seems out of the ordinary. But it would seem that the Lodge's cash flow was pretty tight. He wasn't losing money, but he wasn't really making anything either. Just barely scraping by.''

''Take a look at his correspondence,'' suggested Sarah.

Harvey exited the financial program, and started the word processor. He then opened the directory and examined the names of the document files.

''Looks like he enjoyed writing letters.'' said Harvey, opening a few of the files and reading the content. ''But all of it is painfully ordinary business stuff.''

''What about this one called 'mast.doc,' '' said Sarah, pointing to the file name on the screen. ''Open that one and see what it says.''

Harvey tried to open the file. A message from the computer appeared instead of the file. ''The file is password protected, naturally. I'll make a copy of it on a floppy disk. Maybe Sheriff Randall knows somebody who can get into it anyway.''

Harvey picked up a blank disk from the stack on the desk, and inserted it into the disk drive.

''I wonder if there are any files referencing other people here at the Lodge,'' said Sarah. Harvey skimmed through the file names and found only one familiar name.

"Here's one," he said. " 'Sgrey.doc,' and it's not password protected."

"What does it say?"

Harvey looked disappointed. "It's just a copy of the letter inviting him to the Lodge."

"But look at the date," Sarah said, pointing.

"Right, that was last year. So Mr. Grey is no stranger to Laurel Springs, or the Lodge. This deal must have been in the works for some time."

"Significant?"

"Maybe. We'll keep it in mind."

Harvey continued to scan the files.

"Oh, look at this, Galen's got an encyclopedia on this computer. Incredible."

"Well, why are you bringing it up? What are you looking for?"

"You'll see. . . ."

In a few seconds, the entry displayed on the screen.

Sarah read, "Diabetes . . . dangers of inadequate care and treatment . . ."

"Ah, here are the two types of critical conditions. . . ."

"Harvey, why are you still on this?"

"I just want to know what happened, dear. Let's see . . . insulin reaction, or hypoglycemia, is the result of an extreme and rapid drop in blood sugar. It can happen quickly, but is just as quickly corrected, and rarely fatal.''

Harvey read to the next entry. ''But the opposite reaction is diabetic coma, a result of extreme and prolonged rises in blood sugar due to too little insulin activity. Untreated, it is almost always fatal.''

''Does it list symptoms?''

''Yes, they're listed here: constant thirst, flushed dry skin, weakness, fatigue and drowsiness, labored breathing, breath has fruity odor, vomiting, and finally unconsciousness.''

Harvey folded his arms, thinking.

''So what do you think?'' asked Sarah.

''Poor Lisa had a history of not taking good care of her condition. If she had recently been taking her shots of insulin erratically, or not at all, maybe she could be pushed into coma by a single traumatic event.''

''Like what?''

''Like someone who knew about her weakened condition could have substituted something else for her insulin.''

''Substituted what? Water?''

''Yes, or maybe even glucagon.''

''Glucagon?''

Harvey pointed to another paragraph on the screen. ''You see, according to this, insulin-dependent diabetics frequently keep glucagon on hand. It's a hormone that does the opposite of insulin—it causes the liver to release more glucose into the bloodstream.''

"Why would a diabetic need that? That seems pretty dangerous."

"If someone took too much insulin by accident, or missed a meal, or something similar, their insulin shots could cause a hypoglycemic condition. The glucagon would stabilize them."

Sarah stood and faced Harvey. "So you're saying someone here deliberately substituted glucagon for Lisa's insulin to induce a fatal coma?"

"It's a possibility. Several of our key suspects have been around this place long enough to know about Lisa's condition. Her insulin and glucagon were just sitting in the refrigerator for anyone to see and tamper with. And what better way to cover up a murder than to make it look like a result of a condition she already suffered from, and was having trouble controlling?"

Sarah sighed. "The question remains, Harvey—why?"

"To get rid of the person who assisted in the murder."

"Harvey, you're not seriously considering that Lisa was actually involved, are you?" Her look was incredulous.

"Only unwittingly. I think the murderer convinced Lisa to do something at eight o'clock. Something quite innocent on the surface. Something even you or I would do without hesitation. But whatever it was, it helped John Galen's murderer."

Sarah thought for a moment, then said, "That may

be a possibility, Harvey, but if we can identify John Galen's killer, the question is irrelevant, isn't it?''

''Hardly. As long as the killer is hidden, we are all in danger. Especially if we get too close. We have to be very careful.''

Helen Roma's face was streaked with mascara as she wiped away tears from her reddened eyes. Sarah sat in the chair next to her in John Galen's office, attempting to comfort her.

''I'm sorry.'' Helen sobbed. ''I told myself I wouldn't carry on like this during the questioning . . . but I can't help it.''

''I quite understand, Miss Roma,'' said Harvey warmly. ''I'll try to keep this as brief as possible. I only need to know a couple of things.''

Harvey toyed with a mechanical pencil sitting on the desk as he spoke. This little habit annoyed Sarah, but it helped Harvey concentrate to play with an object as he talked.

''First of all, Miss Roma, can you tell me how long you knew Mr. Galen, and how long you'd been engaged?''

''I've known John for two years,'' she began. ''We met here. I was vacationing with my sister. There were problems with the room, and we had called for the manager, and there was John. A big teddy bear, I remember thinking. But despite his booming voice, and his size, he seemed such a kind man, and a helpful one, too. He made everything right about the room. I don't know why we had dinner together that evening; it just seemed to be one of those things that happen. You know, just being in the right place at the right time, like fate.''

''I'm not sure I believe in 'fate' as such, Miss Roma.''

''No, I don't suppose you would, Reverend. Well, call it what you like, divine appointment, or whatever. Anyway, we just hit it off right away. I must confess I fell in love immediately.''

''And he felt the same way?''

''Not at first. I mean, he liked me very much, and we saw each other off and on for several months. But I always got the impression that he still saw other women also. Not that he ever said so, but I just felt that he did. No real commitment, if you get my meaning.''

''Did this bother you?''

''Yes, it did, actually. I know that he had no real obligation to me; we weren't officially steady or anything. But I'm rather old-fashioned, and wanted to be the only one.''

Harvey leaned forward with his elbows on the desk, as Helen mangled her handkerchief.

''And did you tell him this?''

''I did. One night we were having dinner together. I asked him if he'd seen other women while he was seeing me. He said he had, but nothing serious. It's strange—I felt so betrayed. Even though we were only casually dating, I couldn't bear to think of him with anyone else. I told him so.''

''Was he mad?''

''Not at all. I was surprised how understanding he was about it. He apologized for his casual approach to our relationship, and asked me to be his steady girlfriend. I said yes before he could get the words out of his mouth.''

''And your engagement?''

''We dated for over a year. He only asked me to marry him four months ago. I was so excited. We had such plans. Then when he talked about selling the Lodge, and all the money he would have, and all the things we could do together, traveling the world and all . . .''

Helen's restraint began to break down again and the tears resumed.

''I'm sorry,'' she said, ''I can't believe he's gone. It's like a dream—if only I could wake from it. I've tried not to think about him. I even stopped wearing my engagement ring because it was a constant reminder. But everywhere I look, all I see is John. This place was truly his . . . it bears his very personality. Reverend Ashe, I do hope we can get through this soon, and go home. I don't know how long I can bear this.''

Sarah patted Helen's cold hand as Harvey stood up.

''I'll do everything I can, Miss Roma. You have my

word. Just two quick questions, and we'll be through. Just where were you when John was . . . attacked?''

Harvey pointed toward the blueprints on the desk. Helen stood up and leaned over the desk, trying to see the fading lines through the veil of tears in her burning eyes.

''I was here, in John's office, on the phone.''

''Oh, yes,'' said Harvey, ''I remember, you got a phone call just after dinner. I had to use the phone also and had to wait for you to get off the phone to clear the line.''

Helen looked perplexed, pointing toward the phone on the desk. ''That's strange. There are two lines, and I only used one. Who was on the other line?''

Harvey remembered that *both* lines were busy when he tried to use the phone.

''What does it mean, Harvey?'' said Sarah. ''Is it important?''

''I don't see how. Miss Roma, were you in here all the time?''

''Yes, until I hung up the phone. Then I joined everyone else in the dining room. I think I was sitting in that big chair by the fireplace.''

Harvey leaned forward with his elbows on the desk.

''Miss Roma, what do you know about Lisa Aames?''

''The desk clerk?'' She looked surprised at the question.

''Yes.''

"Well, I've never really paid much attention to John's hourly employees. I've seen her around, and I know John thought a lot of her."

"Is that all?"

Helen's brow creased as she thought hard. "I only remember John remarking about how much she was out sick. I remember thinking it was strange that he was so pleased with her as an employee, since she was so undependable. But then that was none of my business."

"Did you know she was diabetic?"

"No, I did not," Helen responded immediately.

"Okay, one last thing, Miss Roma. Does the name Clarckston mean anything to you?"

"Why, no, not at all."

"Thank you, Miss Roma, you've been most helpful. You can go now."

Helen nodded and moved toward the door. "Reverend, I know this is difficult for you, being a preacher and having to get involved with all this. I appreciate you being here, and I'm glad it's you investigating this case."

"Thank you for your patience. I hope after all this is over that you will feel free, perhaps, to see me for counseling. I have a bit more experience there than in crime detection. Maybe with some spiritual guidance we can get you through this trying time."

"Thank you, Reverend, I'll do that."

Helen walked quietly out of the office, closing the door behind her. Sarah sat down, exasperated.

''This is getting us nowhere, Harvey. No one here seems to have motive or opportunity for this killing. I'm afraid I'm baffled.''

Harvey slid into the chair beside Sarah, taking her hand.

''Baffled? You? I can't believe it!''

Sarah smiled. ''I can assure you, it's a temporary condition.''

Harvey nodded, and said seriously, ''For everyone's sake, I hope so.''

Chapter Six

"Jessica," Floyd said, bringing a stack of dirty dishes to the counter, "what do you think will happen now? What will happen to the Lodge, to all of us who work here?"

Jessica was scrubbing forcefully with steel wool, trying desperately to clean the pan she held. She sighed, pushing a lock of brown hair from her sweating face, and rested momentarily from her labor. Despite the cold outside, the kitchen was steamy from the hot water as they washed dishes.

"Up until last night I would have said we're all out of a job, Floyd," Jessica said, resuming her scrubbing. "But now, everything's changed. I guess now the Lodge will remain, and maybe so will we."

Floyd picked up a dish from the dirty stack and

dipped it into the hot soapy water. "Did John have any family that you know of?"

"Yes, back in Philadelphia, no one around here."

"Then how do you know the Lodge will stay? Whoever inherits it is liable to sell it to Scott Grey just like John would have."

"I don't think that's likely, Floyd."

"Why not?"

"Well, I happen to know that there were special stipulations in the sales contract when John bought the place. Unless John had a will, which knowing him, I doubt, the Lodge goes back to the estate of the original owner."

Floyd put down his dirty dish, looking at Jessica with surprise.

"Why would John agree to such a strange condition as that? You would think he would want to control what happened to the Lodge in the event of his death."

"John knew the family that used to own it. They were actually a bit wary about selling it outside the family. They didn't want it to end up belonging to some hotel chain, or some big corporation. John respected that, and knowing he was unmarried, had no children, and didn't really get along well with his own family, he agreed to it."

"But if he made a will?"

"It would have superseded the condition on the sales contract, but I don't think he did. It wasn't his way. A will would have taken too much planning, too much thinking ahead. It was a bit out of his league, if you know what I mean. Besides, he acted as though he would live forever.''

''I guess the old owners' family was shocked when they heard he was going to sell.''

''I don't think they knew. Until last night, no one except John and Mr. Grey knew about it. But I think the Clarckstons would have objected, yes.''

''You knew them?''

''Yes, you could say that.''

Floyd was rinsing the plates he had just washed. ''It'll be good to know the Lodge will stay. I'd hate to be unemployed.''

''Floyd, you're such a good chef. I don't think you'd have any trouble finding work elsewhere. John told me your last restaurant was a four-star establishment in Philadelphia. I'm sure they'd be glad to have you back. I'm surprised they ever allowed someone to snatch you away. Come to think of it, I'm surprised you'd have even come for what John could afford to pay you. Why did you come, Floyd?''

Floyd dropped a plate from his soapy hands. The crash startled Jessica.

''Oh, Jessica!'' he grunted. ''I'm sorry. It's not like me to drop a dish. Oh . . . let me go get a broom.''

Floyd dried his hands on his apron as he walked to the pantry to find a broom. Jessica squatted to the floor and began picking up the larger shards. Floyd returned in a moment with the broom, and began sweeping the fragments.

"I've not been myself today, Jessica," Floyd explained. "I just can't get over all this. First John, and then this morning to see poor Lisa dead . . ."

"You and Lisa were good friends, weren't you?"

"She was like a daughter to me. You know, her father had died a couple of years ago, and she kind of looked up to me. I'm the one who convinced her to apply for this job. I guess I feel responsible for what happened."

"Floyd," Jessica touched his arm with encouragement. "You couldn't possibly have known any of this would happen. You can't blame yourself for something that happened because of her own carelessness with her medicine."

"Jessica, you heard what Reverend Ashe said upstairs this morning. He didn't think it was an accident, or her carelessness. He suspected something more. If that dear girl was murdered while working here, I'd never forgive myself."

"Floyd, believe me, you are not responsible, whatever happened to her."

"You don't understand." Floyd's voice was weak with grief. "Lisa never took her condition seriously. She thought she was too young to suffer consequences. I never should have done it."

"Done what?" asked Jessica.

He looked up at her guiltily. "Lisa came to the

kitchen yesterday during her break. I was making the cheesecake and she begged me for a piece. She sure loved cheesecake. I know it was bad for her, but I just couldn't say no. She took a big piece upstairs to have after supper. She said she'd just take an extra insulin shot, as if that would make it all right. I should have said no. But I didn't.''

''Floyd, it was not your responsibility. I know what I'm talking about.''

Floyd emptied the dustpan into the trash, the fragments making a clattering sound as they fell. Jessica glanced toward the window as she scrubbed. The light was getting dim outside as dusk approached. It looked as if the entire world had disappeared, and the Lodge was all that remained. It made Jessica feel very lonely, very depressed.

''Floyd,'' she asked softly, ''what are you and the mayor involved in?''

Floyd did not even look at Jessica. He was scrubbing the dried spaghetti sauce from the stove.

''What do you mean, Jessica?''

''I overheard Mayor Halon talking to Mr. Mast today. I know they're up to something underhanded; I could tell by the way they were talking. They mentioned you.''

Floyd shook his head, continuing to scrub. ''I can't imagine, Jessica. I've never even talked to the mayor other than when he's here, and then only casually.''

''Yes, but he comes here a lot, doesn't he?''

"He likes it here. He entertains business associates here all the time. You know, trying to attract business to the town. Jessica, it seems that you're suspicious of everyone. You've managed to point the finger at me, at Lisa, at the mayor. Why don't you just relax and let Reverend Ashe do his job?"

"You're right, Floyd," she said as she wiped the counter. "I'm just a little edgy, too. I'm sorry, I just need to stop thinking about it."

"Yes, now that we're through with cleaning up after lunch, it's time to start thinking about dinner."

Dinner was a very quiet affair that evening. Floyd, in no mood for elaborate fare, had simply warmed up a stew that had been in the freezer. It was not much, but under the trying circumstances, no one seemed to mind.

They had all dined together, although the meal turned out to be a silent one. After dinner, they gathered once again before the fireplace. This was not planned at all; it seemed only that there was safety in numbers. Coffee and hot tea were flowing; the fire was crackling. Harvey was staring into the fire, deep in thought.

"Harvey . . . Harvey . . ."

Harvey blinked as he returned from his mental wandering.

"I'm sorry . . . honey, did you say something?"

"Harvey, Mr. Halon has asked you a question. Did

you even hear him?'' said Sarah, nudging Harvey's elbow.

''I'm sorry, Mayor,'' Harvey said. ''I wasn't listening, I must confess. What did you say?''

Mayor Halon seemed irritated that Harvey had ignored him, but continued.

''Reverend, I just wanted to know how things were going. We went through an entire dinner. And now we've been sitting here for twenty minutes without a word. All of us are dying—sorry—very curious to know what you've found out.''

Harvey sipped his coffee. ''Mr. Halon, we've found out a great deal of information. How valuable it is to the case is yet to be determined. As I'm sure you can appreciate, ninety percent of the testimony one hears in these cases is extraneous. The key is determining just what is and what isn't.''

''Any conclusions yet?'' asked Jim Mast, leaning against the mantel.

''I have a few notions, but I'd prefer to keep them to myself just now.''

''What do we do now?'' asked Halon.

''I still need to speak with a few of you, as you know. Once I have everyone's story, perhaps something will begin to make sense.''

''So you would agree that none of this makes sense?'' asked Scott Grey.

''Of course not. I'd be disappointed if the killer made it too easy.''

"Your levity astounds me, Reverend," said Benjamin Barten.

Harvey looked at Barten with piercing eyes. "Not levity, Mr. Barten, but recognition of a certain degree of cunning. In my days as a police detective, I encountered dozens of murders. Mostly senseless acts of violence related to drugs and organized crime. But it's been a long time since I saw a case such as this, where a murder was planned and executed in this way. Most murders are solved by simple persistence and good police work. Not this kind. What we have here demands a higher level of deduction than—"

"Would you listen to yourselves!" cried Helen belligerently. "Two people are dead. And you ramble on as if this were some puzzle to solve, some clever game to play. This is no parlor game!"

Harvey put down his cup and stood before Helen.

"You are very correct, Miss Roma," he assured. "If I offend you in any way, I'm deeply sorry. My point is not to diminish the vileness of this murder. I am simply pointing out the approach we must take. This is a trying situation. We are cut off, isolated. There is likely a murderer among us, who may strike again. We tend to panic in these situations, just as you are. However natural that may be in trying times, we have to keep our heads. We cannot let emotions cloud our judgment or allow us to carelessly overlook something. This could be deadly, you understand. You used the word 'puzzle.' This is somewhat accurate. But all puzzles have a solution, and we *will* find it.''

Helen took a few deep breaths, looking down at the floor, reaching for her hot tea from the end table.

''Yes, you're right, of course, Reverend. That's two emotional outbursts in one day. You must think me hopeless.''

''Not at all, Miss Roma, quite forgivable given our mutual plight, and your loss. Please believe me, I'm trying to help. I did not ask to be involved in this, but I am. We must make the best of it.''

After his short sermon, Harvey returned to his chair, watching the fire. His coffee had begun to cool off, but Sarah alertly grabbed the coffeepot from the table and filled his cup for him.

After a few silent and awkward minutes, casual conversation began to return. Ben Barten shared what he heard on the radio about the weather to Mast and Halon. The blizzard was expected to continue for at least another day before dissipating. Sarah had once again taken to comforting Helen, who seemed to be having a difficult time with this crisis. Jessica and Julie made small talk about really nothing at all.

As before, Harvey's mind was not on casual talk. He could think only of woodsheds, of telephones, of sharp objects. He did not know exactly how long he was in his trance, but a loud pop from the fire brought him back to the present. He looked at his watch, and realized it was approaching 7:00. He wanted to question the last few people before retiring for the night, and the night was going fast. He stood up.

"Excuse me," he said to stop the hum of conversation. "I hate to say this, but I feel we must continue with the process of questioning. I'd like to get this behind us tonight. Mr. Helton, if you'd be so indulgent as to see me in Mr. Galen's office, I have just a few questions."

Floyd timidly followed Harvey and Sarah into the office, where Harvey asked a few perfunctory questions about Floyd's whereabouts at the time of the murder. Floyd was, of course, simply running back and forth between the kitchen and the dining room during that time. With all the chaos going on, anyone could have slipped through the kitchen and out the back door, if they were watching Floyd's movements carefully. He remembered seeing some slushy footprints on the kitchen floor, but assumed these were made by Mr. Galen returning with the wood. He had not realized at the time that Mr. Galen had never returned. Floyd had not talked to Lisa Aames at all the previous evening, and did not ask her to stay overnight at the Lodge. He had no idea who would have done so.

In the dining room, Halon and Mast had huddled together away from the others, whispering among themselves. As each minute passed with Floyd talking to Harvey, Jim Mast seemed more upset. The mayor continued to reassure him, to no avail.

"I think you should go in there and see what's going on," urged Mast.

"Are you nuts?" the mayor replied. "I can't just go barging in like that. I've already told you, it will be all right. Floyd won't be a—"

Halon stopped as he heard the door open in Galen's office. Floyd Helton emerged, appearing somewhat ragged. He nodded to Harvey, who was standing just inside the door, and went up the stairs. Harvey turned and looked toward Jim Mast, and motioned for him to come.

"Don't worry, Jim," repeated the mayor. "Just answer his questions."

Mast nodded, but was lightly perspiring as he walked shakily toward the office. Mast hated that smile on Harvey's face. He hated anyone who smiled all the time. He didn't care too much for preachers either. Harvey Ashe was the worst of both.

"Just relax, Mr. Mast," said Harvey, patting Mast's shoulder as he showed him to the chair. "No one is accusing anyone of anything. We're just trying to get the facts of the case. You only need to tell me the truth about what you remember. Okay?"

Mast nodded silently, but flinched when Sarah activated the recorder.

"Now, Mr. Mast," began Harvey, "I understand you are the president of the local Chamber of Commerce."

"That's right."

"Exactly what business are you in? The Chamber is not an occupation as I understand it, but a professional organization of business leaders."

"That's right, I serve in a voluntary capacity for the Chamber. I own a small chain of pharmacies in the county."

"Would that be the ones called Mountain Apothecary?"

"Yes, that's the one."

"I've given you plenty of business this last couple of years, Mr. Mast. I hope you appreciate it."

Mast smiled slightly. "Of course, we always appreciate loyal customers."

"Mr. Mast, are you actually a pharmacist?"

Mast looked down into his lap. "I haven't actually practiced in many years. I did start out doing just that. I ran the whole thing in the beginning. But now, I'm just a businessman."

"Surely you remember the basics?"

"Of course."

"Well, I'm just curious. This doesn't really have anything to do with you, but since you're the closest thing to a medical expert we have . . ."

Mast looked up defensively. "Yes?"

Harvey produced Lisa's blood sugar machine in a plastic bag from a drawer of the desk, and held it up so that Mast could see the display.

"When I push this button," Harvey said, "it always displays this number. Do you know what it means?"

"Well, what you have there is part of a blood sugar monitoring kit for a diabetic. The number is the blood sugar level. Most of the monitors display the last reading taken for comparison."

"How would you characterize this reading?"

"622? Dangerously high. I'd get to a doctor. It's a potentially lethal level."

Harvey put the monitor down.

"Thanks for the information. That's very helpful. Now, to change the subject a bit, just what is your relationship with Mayor Halon?"

"Just friends. He was a banker years ago before getting into politics. He was my banker, and so we go way back."

"I see. Mr. Mast, do you have any business relationships with anyone else here at the Lodge?"

Mast shook his head. "No, no one here now."

Harvey leaned back in the large chair and locked his fingers together in thought.

"Mr. Mast, what do you know about Floyd Helton?"

Mast sniffed nervously. "Floyd Helton . . . you mean the cook?"

"Yes."

"Well, nothing. I mean, I've seen him around town, and I've seen him when I was here at the Lodge. But I don't really know him, not to speak to him or anything . . . Why do you ask?"

"No reason in particular. It's just routine in these

matters to determine who knows whom, who may have a bone to pick with whom, and so on.''

''He's just a cook, for crying out loud . . .''

Harvey raised his eyebrow.

Mast was visibly rattled. ''I'm sorry . . . I'm just trying to cooperate, Reverend.''

''I know. One last thing, Mr. Mast, why did you go outside after dinner?''

''What? Did I?''

''Yes, I saw you go out the front door about the same time John Galen had gone out the kitchen door.''

''Oh, I remember, I went out to smoke a cigarette. This is a nonsmoking environment, you know. It had been a while, and I needed a smoke.''

''You went outside to smoke—in a blizzard?''

''I told you, I really needed a smoke.''

''I'll bet it was hard to light a cigarette in sixty-mile-an-hour winds.''

''Yes, as a matter of fact it was. But the overhang in front of the lobby shielded me somewhat.''

''You were out there a long time.''

''I know, but I was only smoking.''

''Curious, you say you could barely make it through dinner without smoking, yet I haven't seen you light up all afternoon.''

''Well, like I said, I can't smoke in here, and I just didn't want to go outside in this storm again. It's not worth it.''

Harvey was silent a moment, just looking at Mast.

Harvey never blinked during this, and it severely unnerved Mr. Mast.

"Well, why are you staring at me like that? Don't you believe me?"

"I'm reserving judgment."

"Well, yes, I had time to run around the building and I had time to kill Galen and get back to the dining room. But why would I? What possible motive would I have? I hardly knew him."

"I don't know, what motive *do* you have?"

"None, I assure you."

"Would Floyd Helton say the same?"

"Floyd wouldn't say . . ." Mast stopped before he said anything further, standing defiantly.

"I think we've talked long enough. Perhaps I should save my comments for the real police."

"Suit yourself, Mr. Mast. That's all I have."

The smile returned to Harvey's face as he extended a hand. "Thank you for your cooperation."

Disarmed by pleasantness, Mast returned the handshake. "I'm sorry I lost my temper, Reverend. I'm not used to this. I've never been in the middle of something like this before. You'll have to be patient with us all."

"Of course, Mr. Mast. Oh, by the way, I did want to ask one simple yes-or-no question. Do you know anyone named Clarckston?"

Mast considered the question for a moment before replying, ''No, the name is totally unfamiliar. Should I know it?''

''Probably not. Thank you again.''

Chapter Seven

"Harvey, I think we've gotten ourselves in the middle of something very strange," noted Sarah with a worried look on her face. "After what Jessica told us about the mayor and Mr. Mast's conversation, I just don't know what to think. Jim Mast acted very frightened just then."

"I agree," said Harvey. "Floyd admitted to us how often those two are here, sometimes at odd hours for so-called business meetings."

"But if Jessica is telling the truth about Floyd being mentioned in their conversation, Floyd may be involved himself."

"Yes, but we heard that secondhand from Jessica herself. We have to bear the source in mind. Jessica could also be involved in whatever is going on. John Galen might very well have been in on it, too.''

''What could it all be about?''

''Some shady business dealings, I'd guess. Clearly, someone here at the Lodge is a part of it. I do think that Floyd Helton is the key to it.''

''You need to see me next?'' asked Mayor Halon, just coming in the door of the office.

Harvey motioned for him to sit down. Halon was smiling in an artificial way as he took a seat.

''What do you want to know, Reverend?'' Halon offered with a helpful tone in his voice.

''Anything that's likely to be helpful, Mr. Halon.''

''I'll do what I can, of course.''

''I'm interested in your business relationship with John Galen, and with Jim Mast.''

The smile disappeared from the mayor's face very abruptly. ''What does Jim have to do with it?''

''Probably nothing, but we have to explore all avenues of discussion, you know.''

Halon shifted in his chair, and began stroking the five-o'clock shadow on his chin.

''Jim and I have cooperated in various business and personal projects for years. We are good friends. I did not know Mr. Galen personally. He has been very gracious in hosting many meetings and conferences here. In a small town, it is part of the mayor's job to work hard to attract business and industry. The Lodge is a very hospitable place to bring people, usually.''

''I suppose that Floyd has been very helpful in setting up and serving at your meetings, hasn't he?''

''Floyd? Oh, you mean Helton, the cook. Yes, he's helped us out some.''

''Have you known him long?''

''I don't really know him at all. Like Mr. Galen, he's just someone who works here, and I come here from time to time. I recognize him as an employee, and that's about it.''

Harvey rose from his chair quietly, and found himself standing at the small window. The only sound Mayor Halon could hear was the soft whirring of the recorder, and the constant wind beating on the Lodge.

''Um . . . Reverend,'' the mayor said after a few moments of silence, ''was there anything else? Are we through?''

''Almost, Mayor,'' replied Harvey. ''Would you mind telling me why you went upstairs after dinner?''

''I . . . needed to go back to my room for a few minutes . . . if you get my drift.''

Harvey turned back toward Halon, leaning back against the windowsill with his arms crossed.

''There's a men's room down here in the lobby, you know.''

''Yes, I'm aware of that. I rather had the impression it was very busy at that moment, so I just went upstairs.''

"Did you know about the fire escapes from the upstairs rooms?"

"Fire escapes? I'd never really noticed them."

"Well, there are. On your floor, the fire escape brings you right by the kitchen door."

"Really?"

"Yes, really."

Harvey was now looking directly into Halon's eyes.

"Reverend Ashe, I honestly did not know it was there."

"Did anyone see you go into your room?"

"No."

"And you were gone how long?"

"Maybe fifteen minutes. Plenty of time to rush down the fire escape I knew nothing about, and brave the blizzard winds to kill John Galen for no reason at all, and still manage to make it back up the fire escape and back to dining room, with no sign of ever having been outside in the weather."

"It would be quite a feat, I agree. But surely not beyond your inestimable capabilities."

"I suppose. But why would I?"

Harvey walked back to the desk and sat on its edge as he continued.

"Perhaps you are related to the Clarckstons?"

"Clarckstons? I really have no idea who they are. What do they have to do with this case?"

"Maybe nothing. Mayor, the Lodge is a very important institution for you, in a business sense, isn't it?''

''Well, yes, I suppose it is. As I've said before, it brings tourists and is a good place for business meetings and so forth.''

''I guess you'd hate to see it close down.''

''It wouldn't be the end of the world, Reverend. Certainly not worth someone's life. I think, Reverend, you are stretching the point here. I wouldn't kill for a hotel.''

''Sometimes people kill to protect a secret, though, don't they?''

''Some people might. I wouldn't. Especially since I have no secret to hide. I'm just a small-town mayor trying to do his job.''

''Yes, of course. Well, Mayor, I thank you for your time. I'll see you in the morning.''

The mayor nodded and left the room. Harvey sat down again, picking up the recorder. The soft click of the OFF button seemed loud in the still-silent room. Harvey ejected the microcassette, and toyed with it as he thought.

''Harvey,'' Sarah said, breaking the silence, ''I think you're getting tired. We all are. None of us are thinking clearly, and I think we all need rest.''

''Sarah, if I could just sort through all this information, and see some pattern, some trail I could follow.''

''Harvey,'' she said, stroking his strong hand,

"dear, you'll think more clearly in the morning. I think tempers in there are getting short. Let's call it a night."

Harvey sighed. "Maybe you're right. I *am* very tired. My eyelids feel like sandpaper. I guess we're not as young as we once were, are we, 'old dear'?"

Sarah stood up, leading him to the door. "Speak for yourself, 'old dear,' I, for one, am just getting started!"

Harvey and Sarah, arm in arm, came back to the fireplace area where the rest of the party waited. Helen Roma was flipping absently through a three-year-old fishing magazine. Clearly, she was not even comprehending what she was reading. Her gray eyes seemed to be focused on another reality, not at all on the place where she was. Jim Mast was pacing behind the sofa. Scott Grey had dozed off in the chair. Jessica returned from the kitchen with a soft drink.

"I think it's time we retired for the evening," Harvey announced as all eyes were upon him. "It's been a long day, we are all on edge and exhausted. Let's get some rest and continue in the morning. Perhaps we'll be lucky and the storm will let up enough for help to arrive, and for us to leave."

"I'm for that," said Mast, picking up his jacket.

"Needless to say," continued Harvey, "I recommend that we remain locked in our rooms until morning."

"What if the murderer has a master key?" said Benjamin Barten.

"Good point," agreed Harvey. "Jessica, how many master keys are there?"

Jessica had just taken a sip of her drink. "I really don't know. This is just a mountain lodge, not a high-security installation. We don't inventory our master keys. Every now and then we have the locks changed, but that hasn't been done in a year or two."

"Where are they kept?"

"In a drawer under the cash register at the front desk."

"So anyone could have taken one?"

"I suppose so."

"Well, all the same, I think it would be a good idea to secure all the ones you know about, including your own."

"I agree," said the mayor. "And I think that you should keep them, Reverend."

"Me? I don't think that's wise. No one, you see, is above suspicion at this time."

"I think you're the only one everybody trusts, Reverend," said Jessica. "After all, you and Sarah were the only ones in complete view of everyone all the time, during the killing. You're the only one who really could not have committed the murder. You're the logical choice."

Harvey had to agree with Jessica's reasoning. It was

put to a vote and decided unanimously that Harvey would keep all the passkeys.

Harvey stood and watched as the last of the coffee cups were cleared away, the lights in the dining room were turned off, and Floyd checked the fireplace one last time to see that the flames were out.

It had indeed been a long day for the Ashes. As Harvey unlocked the door to their room and walked inside, he felt a strange feeling of release. He sat down on the bed, kicking off his shoes. Even though it was only a hotel room, he felt as if it were his temporary sanctuary. He had not realized until that moment how much pressure he had accepted. At first it had been exhilarating being involved in a murder case. But now, after a long day of questioning and being stuck in the Lodge with no place to go, he began to remember why police work had gotten to him after all those years. He could tell that all the other guests resented him for his relentless inquiries. He could tell especially that the mayor and Jim Mast took great exception to his being in charge. All the same, he knew that he must see it through, and complete his task. He missed home, and he missed Ulysses.

Closing his eyes, Harvey took in a long, deep breath to relax his frayed nerves. Sarah had just come out of the bathroom in her silky, mint-green nightgown, which flowed behind her as if it were being blown in a breeze.

"Harvey, you need to get comfortable and get in that bed. You're exhausted," said Sarah.

"I know, dear, but I'm too keyed up to sleep. I think I'll just read a few minutes, and maybe I'll get sleepy."

"That's probably a good idea. But I'm sleepy. I hope you don't mind if I go ahead and lie down."

"No, of course not. Go on to sleep. I'm sure I won't be far behind you."

"I'm sure, too. I've never known you to be able to read for more than fifteen minutes at night before you're out."

Harvey laughed quietly, got up, and opened his briefcase. He took out his Bible, and sat up in bed and began to read.

The hour had gotten late. Sarah was sound asleep. Her deep and even breathing was relaxing and soothing to Harvey. The Lodge was very silent. It was a strained, frightened silence. But why wouldn't it be? After all, somewhere in this place was a murderer, and his victims, and a fearful, fretful group of people trying not to *become* victims.

Harvey had time to think, and to sort out the barrage of information he had collected during the day. Several times he had stopped reading and put on headphones to listen to parts of the tapes of the interviews from the day, trying to remember little details. Then he would resume his reading. He felt bad that his mind kept wandering from the text he was reading, but it was as if he could think of nothing else.

Harvey put his Bible on the nightstand and looked over to see if Sarah was still asleep. He stood up and put on his shoes. As quietly as he could he walked over to the door. As his hand touched the doorknob, he heard rustling.

"Harvey," a sleepy voice said, "where are you going? Why aren't you in bed?"

"I thought you were asleep, dear."

"I was until you touched that door."

"How could my touching this door wake you up?"

"I don't know, Harvey, women just know when their husbands are about to do something stupid."

"How do you know what I'm going to do?"

"I don't, but it must be stupid if you have to do it in the middle of the night while I'm asleep."

"With your powers of deduction, *you* should be the detective, dear."

Sarah sat up in bed.

"Well, what are you about to do?"

Harvey turned and walked back over to the bed.

"I just need to check out a few things, when no one else is around."

"What things?"

"I want to look around in the kitchen, and so forth."

Sarah gave him the look that indicated she knew he had other intentions.

"And what else, Harvey?"

"I want to look at the bodies again, okay?"

Sarah was standing, reaching for her robe. "Why is it so important, and why can't it wait until tomorrow?"

"Sarah, I just can't sleep, and I've got ideas running around in my head, and things I want to check out. Like I said, it'll just be easier to look around without distraction if I do it now."

"Well, if you think it's that important . . ."

"I do."

Sarah reached for her dress which was draped across the back of the chair.

"I'm sorry I called your intentions 'stupid.' "

"Honey, where are you going?"

"I'm coming with you."

"Sarah, I think you should stay here."

"I'd rather be with you."

"Even on a stupid escapade?"

"It won't be stupid if *I* go, dear."

"All right, let's go and get it over with so we can get back and get some sleep."

Harvey had found a flashlight behind the front desk, and the two of them were skulking through the darkened kitchen. The downstairs rooms had taken on a distinct chilliness in the night.

"What exactly are we looking for?"

"The murder weapon. I'm convinced it's somewhere in here."

"Why?"

"I think the killer went out through that door," he said, pointing to the door leading outside from the kitchen, "and came back in the same way. The weapon could be picked up, cleaned off, and replaced very easily and quickly."

Harvey shined the light around various parts of the kitchen. Large metal pots hung from hooks above the island in the center of the kitchen. Another row of hooks on the wall above the counter held ladles and spatulas and other assorted implements. Sarah opened a couple of drawers. They all contained various cooking utensils and tools, some of them quite large and lethal-looking.

"What about this, Harvey?" Sarah said, holding up a large metal meat tenderizer. "In the right hands this thing could be pretty deadly."

Harvey came over to the counter where Sarah stood and took the implement from her.

"Yes, I'd say it could be lethal, but the shape just doesn't match. But we'll take it with us."

"Where?"

"To match it against the wound on the back of Galen's head—I took pictures of everything."

"Oh, that's right. I was hoping you wouldn't say that."

"The truth is, Sarah, that almost anything in this kitchen could be used for such a purpose. But for the most part, they're all just too blunt to inflict the wound

Galen has. Nothing here is sharp enough other than a knife. And his wound is definitely not a stab wound, it's an impact wound.''

''So you don't think it's here?''

''I don't know, dear. Let's go on downstairs and take a look at the pictures. And I want to check on the body in the refrigerator, too.''

There had been a few lights on in the lobby, but the staircase leading downstairs was completely dark. As they rounded the curved staircase, it opened into a large black space. Harvey shined his light into the convention room, but its light seemed to be swallowed up by the darkness. Sarah was clutching his arm tightly as they walked into the room, and he felt as if his circulation were being cut off. He panned the light around and found the door marked PANTRY. He tested the door, and it was locked.

''Now what do you do?'' said Sarah.

Harvey held up his hand and a key ring jangled in the light.

''Harvey, where did you get them?''

''Behind the front desk, next to the flashlight. I thought they might come in handy.''

''You're just incredible.''

''I know.''

Harvey started trying various keys from the tremendous key ring.

''Naturally, they have a hundred keys and none of them are labeled,'' complained Harvey.

"Tribulation worketh patience, dear."

"Then I'm developing lots of patience this weekend."

At last, the correct key slid into the lock, and the pantry door swung open revealing a large storage room. At the rear of the room was the door to the walk-in freezer. Harvey aimed the light at the door. It reflected back into his eyes from the shiny steel surface. A padlock dangled from the hasp sealing the unit.

Against the left wall stood a large wooden cabinet with double doors. There was also a lock on this cabinet.

"I wonder what's in there," said Harvey, again fumbling through the keys.

"I'm sure it's just more supplies, Harvey. I thought you wanted to look at the body."

"I do, Sarah, but I need to examine all . . . possibilities, you know."

Sarah held the light for Harvey as he successively tried each key in the lock. No key on the ring was the correct one.

"Somehow I suspected as much," concluded Harvey.

"Are you sure you didn't miss one?"

"I'm positive. But perhaps John Galen has the key on his person. Let's go on to the freezer and finish this task."

Harvey turned his attention to the freezer door.

"Here, Sarah, hold the light," he said as he fumbled through the keys for the padlock key. Upon finding a likely candidate, Harvey pushed it into the lock and turned. A dull click came from the body of the padlock as it dropped open. Harvey moved the hasp and turned the large silver handle of the freezer, standing back as the door swung open.

Sarah stood back as a blast of frozen air escaped from inside. Harvey took the light and started toward the door. Sarah hesitated in the storage room.

"Are you okay, dear?" Harvey asked, noticing her reluctance. "You know you don't have to do this."

"I know, Harvey," she replied. "I said I would come with you and I will. It's just that I've never been with a dead body . . . like this . . . I mean, I've been to many funerals, but you know—this person hasn't been . . . prepared."

"I know, it's probably not going to be pretty. You can stay out here if you want."

"No, as long as I'm with you I'll be all right. Let's go and get it over with."

She took Harvey's hand, and together they entered the freezer. The small unit was not much larger than a closet. Both sides were lined with shelves, filled with various frozen foods. On the floor was the second victim, covered with sheets.

"Are you ready?" Harvey warned.

"Yes, go ahead."

Harvey pulled back the sheet to reveal Lisa's face.

Her death had not been of a violent nature, and Lisa looked only asleep. Sarah's detachment weakened, and she shed a small tear.

"Sarah, could you look out in the storage room and see if you can find a small bag of some kind? In case I find something," Harvey said.

Nodding affirmatively Sarah stood up and went out into the storage room. She set the flashlight down on a shelf as she rummaged through various items looking for a bag. Soon she found a box of sandwich bags that she assumed would fulfill the requirements. She took them back inside the freezer and handed a bag to Harvey.

Abruptly, they were in complete darkness. Harvey's ears popped as the pressure changed. The door had slammed shut.

"Harvey!" Sarah gasped.

"Sarah," he said in the icy darkness, "the flashlight, where is it?"

"Oh, Harvey, I left it on the shelf in the storage room!"

"All right, don't panic, I'll feel my way to the door."

"But Harvey, I didn't shut it."

"Well, it must have swung to on its own. Doors do that sometimes, you know."

Harvey stood up, and began groping his way along the shelving to the door. He turned the handle and pushed. The handle turned, but the door did not move.

"What's the matter, Harvey?"

"The door won't open."

"Why not?"

"Either it jammed, or . . ."

Sarah stood up in the darkness. Harvey seemed to know she stood, and moved his gaze upward.

"Or someone locked it from outside!" inferred Sarah.

"Now, Sarah," said Harvey as he felt his way back to her, and held her. "Don't jump to conclusions. This building is very old, and if it shut by accident it could have jammed. The excess condensation from having it open so long may have frozen it shut."

"You don't really believe that, do you, Harvey?"

"No, but it sounded good, you know."

"What do we do now? We'll freeze to death in here. With the door closed it's getting colder." She shivered.

"The compressor just kicked on. I think the thermostat was lowered. In this small space we'll suffocate if we don't freeze to death."

"Harvey, where are you going?" called Sarah, feeling him leaving her clutch. In a moment she heard him beating on the door.

"Hello!" he yelled. "Is anyone out there!?"

"Harvey, if someone locked us in here I doubt they'll answer you."

"I guess you're right."

Sarah wrapped her arms tightly around herself as

she felt a wave of frigid air descending on her. As she turned and moved toward the door she accidentally bumped her foot against the lifeless body. This brought a chill to her soul as she was reminded of what was trapped in the freezer with them. Suddenly, she imagined herself lying lifeless beside it.

''Harvey, what are you doing?'' She felt, rather than saw, Harvey move.

Sarah almost fell as she jumped from the sound of a brain-piercing blast. In a moment she heard the door swing open, revealing the forgotten flashlight still on the shelf. Sarah could see the silhouette of Harvey's pistol in the now-open door. The smell of sulfur filled the small room.

''Harvey, you almost scared me to death. Why didn't you warn me you had the pistol?''

''Do you want to stay in here?''

''No, of course not, I'm freezing.''

Harvey held out his hand, and together they moved cautiously into the storage room. Harvey held out his pistol defensively, and grabbed the flashlight shining it all around the convention room. There was no one there.

''Whoever it was is gone now,'' said Harvey. ''I doubt they would stay around long enough to be discovered anyway. Let's check out those keys and see what's behind the mysterious door.''

Harvey reentered the closet, handing the light to

Sarah. He finally found a key that slid easily into the cabinet lock and turned. Harvey swung the doors open.

"Would you look at that!" proclaimed Harvey, taking the light from Sarah and aiming it into the cabinet. The deep cabinet was filled to capacity with boxes of playing cards, poker chips, even a small roulette wheel.

"It's a regular casino in there, Harvey," said Sarah.

"Now we know why this place is such a popular place for business meetings. No doubt the mayor has done some entertaining over the years, with Mr. Galen's help."

"And selling the Lodge would cut into that, wouldn't it?" asked Sarah.

"I think it's safe to say that Mayor Halon and his close business associates have a vested interest in keeping the place going. At least until a suitable substitute—"

Harvey quieted suddenly, as he heard footsteps. He closed the cabinet door, relocking it.

"Who's there?" a woman's voice called from behind them. Harvey swung around quickly, the pistol brought to bear on the now-illuminated target.

It was Jessica Barrow.

"Jessica!" said Harvey. "It's Harvey Ashe. What are you doing here?"

"Reverend," she said, holding her hand in front of her face to shield her eyes from the blinding light, "are you all right? I thought I heard a shot."

''How long have you been down here, Jessica?''

''I just ran down the stairs when I heard what sounded like a shot.''

''You heard it from your third-floor room?''

''Well, no, I was in the lobby.''

''Why?''

''To check the fuses, when the power went out.''

''The power went out? When?''

''Just a few minutes ago. I was awake, reading. I just couldn't sleep, you know.''

''Yeah, I know the feeling.''

''The lights just went out. I came down to check the fuse box. I had just groped my way to the bottom of the steps when I heard the shot.''

Harvey continued to hold the pistol in a defensive manner, moving around Jessica toward the staircase.

''Jessica,'' Harvey said, ''do you mean to tell me that you came running down that dark staircase without a flashlight into a room where you thought you heard a gunshot?''

''I know it wasn't smart, but I'm not thinking very clearly these days.''

''Did you hear me calling?''

''Calling? From where?''

Sarah spoke up. ''From the freezer, where someone just locked us in.''

Jessica put her hand down from her face. She wore a puzzled expression. ''The freezer? What were you two doing in the freezer?''

"Just a bit of detection. Exactly what you asked me to do, Miss Barrow," replied Harvey.

"Could you please take that light out of my eyes? It's blinding me."

Harvey allowed the light to aim upward so that Jessica could see them clearly. Her eyes went immediately to the pistol in Harvey's hand.

"Surely, Reverend, you don't think . . . ."

"I don't know what to think, Jessica. All I know is someone locked us in that freezer not five minutes ago, and the first and only person I see in this room is you."

"But really, I just came down here! You must believe me."

"Did you see anyone else down here, or up in the lobby?"

She shook her head, as he expected. "No, no one. But then I wasn't really expecting anyone until I got down here. Someone could easily have ducked into the dining room until I passed by, and I never would have seen them."

"That's true, of course," agreed Harvey, lowering the pistol. "Maybe we should go upstairs and see if we can get the lights back on. I'll feel a lot safer."

"So will I," said Jessica.

"After you," said Harvey, motioning toward the staircase.

Chapter Eight

As Harvey passed through the door at the top of the stairs, and entered the lobby, he could see a light moving around in the dining room. He could also hear someone shuffling around, making noise.

"Shh . . ." whispered Harvey as he turned off his flashlight. "Someone's in the dining room. You two stay here."

Sarah and Jessica nodded, and waited by the door. Harvey moved cautiously through the lobby toward the dining room. He approached the archway entrance, and peeked around the corner.

There he saw Floyd Helton working with the fire, attempting to revive it.

"Floyd," called Harvey as he walked into the room, turning on his flashlight, "what's going on?"

Helton stood up from his crouched position, holding his light toward Harvey.

"Reverend Ashe," he said in surprise. "I didn't expect to see you up and around."

"Nor I you. How long have you been down here?"

Sarah and Jessica were now standing at Harvey's side.

"I came down when the power went out, to see if it was a fuse. But it's not. We've completely lost power. We need to keep this fire going, because it's going to get cold in here."

Harvey approached the warmth of the fire.

"Floyd, did you see anyone else down here?"

"Why, no. At least not until you showed up."

"Well, by now whoever it was could easily be back up in their room."

"Who? What are you talking about?"

"Floyd, someone just tried to kill Sarah and me!"

Floyd was shocked, and sat suddenly in a chair. "No, Reverend! Why would anyone want to harm you? What happened?"

Before Harvey could answer, he heard footsteps coming down the stairs from the rooms. He shined his light toward the lobby to reveal Jim Mast.

"Good morning, Reverend," Mast greeted. "I guess I wasn't the only one unable to sleep."

"It would appear that few of us can. Won't you join us?"

Harvey motioned to the sofa, and Jim Mast obligingly sat down.

"Jessica, under the circumstances I think we should bring the rest of the party back down here. It's quite possible they're all awake anyway. Floyd, perhaps some coffee would help."

"Reverend, could you give me a hand with it?" asked Floyd.

"Well, if you need me," replied Harvey.

"I'll be glad to help you, Mr. Helton," offered Mast. "You don't need to trouble the Reverend."

"It's quite all right, Mr. Mast," assured Harvey. "I don't mind."

Together they strode into the kitchen as Jessica went upstairs to summon the group. Harvey held the flashlight so that Floyd could light the gas stove and begin to boil water for the coffee.

"So what did you want to talk to me about, Floyd?" asked Harvey.

"Why do you think I want to talk to you?"

"Come now, Floyd, you don't need me to make coffee. You must want to say something to me privately."

Floyd was getting coffee cups down and setting them on a tray.

"Well, Reverend, actually there was something I wanted to tell you."

"Yes. I'm listening. . . ."

"I don't know quite how to tell you. I feel as if I'm betraying a friend."

Harvey put his hand on Floyd's shoulder in a reassuring way. "Go ahead, Floyd, say what's on your mind. It may be important."

"I overheard some of the people talking earlier today," said Floyd, taking a deep breath, "while you were in the office questioning everyone. Several had mentioned that you were asking if anyone knew the Clarckstons."

"Yes, and do you know them?"

Floyd shook his head. "No, but I heard Jessica mention their name today. I wasn't paying that much attention, so I didn't really catch everything she said. But I know I heard her mention them. I'm sure she knows who they are."

"Floyd, please try to remember, what exactly were you two discussing when she mentioned it?"

"Let's see." Floyd seemed to look off into space in deep thought. "We were washing up the lunch dishes, and we were talking, I think about our jobs. You know, what was going to happen to the Lodge now that John was dead, and what would happen to us. I think she mentioned the Clarckstons in relation to who might inherit the Lodge."

"Jessica . . ." Harvey stroked his mustache. "And she was the first person I saw when we came out of the freezer. . . ."

"The freezer? You were down in the storage room?"

"Yes, doing some detective work."

Floyd was suddenly rattled.

"Did you find anything?" he said pensively while fumbling with the lid on the instant coffee jar.

"What do you expect I might have found?"

"Just supplies, canned food, and such."

"Do you go in there often?"

"Well, yes. It's our main storage area."

"Ever seen anything unusual in there?"

"Other than a dead body in the freezer?"

Harvey laughed softly. "Yes, other than a dead body."

Floyd shook his head, and returned his attention to his coffee making.

"No, just food and supplies."

"Have you ever been in that cabinet?"

"No, Reverend," Floyd replied vehemently. "Only Mr. Galen is supposed to go in that cabinet."

"Has he ever talked to you about its contents?"

"Never. I assumed it was personal. I never questioned him about it."

"Aren't you curious?"

"No sir, it's really none of my business, you know. I'm just the cook."

"Yes, of course."

"Floyd, do you think you can handle the coffee alone?"

''If you'll hand me the flashlight in that right-hand drawer so I can see what I'm doing after you're gone, then I think I can handle it.''

Harvey complied. ''Okay, I'll rejoin you in a few minutes, and thanks.''

Harvey reached for the key ring again, and unlocked the door from the kitchen to John Galen's office, and went inside.

Once inside, he closed the door behind him, and flashed his light toward the filing cabinet. He went over to it and opened the drawer containing the personnel files, and retrieved Jessica Barrow's file. He placed it on the desk and began flipping through it to the older records in the back. He shined the light onto a particular document. And there he saw the name he knew he had seen other than in the Lodge's sales contract.

''Clarckston . . .'' he mumbled to himself.

Julie was astonished at how different the soft fabric of her bathrobe belt felt, now that it was wound so tightly around her tender neck. Her field of vision was growing blurry, her attacker's face only a dark shape. The bitterly cold wind whipping under the eaves of her balcony could not bite as viciously as the belt dug into her skin. She tried to scream, but the sound of the wind engulfed what little sound she was able to make. Perhaps this was the reason the attacker had pushed her out on to the balcony to accomplish the task. Julie grasped the balcony post, attempting to prevent falling out of the third story. But the attacker pushed harder, and Julie's weakened condition was no match. She realized she was being rolled over the railing as she first lost consciousness, then life.

The attacker had tied the other end of the robe belt to the post. As Julie's body fell, her neck could be heard to gently snap. The attacker watched thoughtfully. Julie's body swung gracefully in the roaring wind. In this weather, her body would not be discovered until morning.

Satisfied, the murderer left Julie's room. Voices could be heard downstairs. In the darkness, a door closed, unheard by anyone.

"Julie is not in her room, Reverend," informed Jessica as Harvey came out of Galen's office.

"Not in her room?" replied Harvey. "Where could she be?"

"I don't know. I knocked on her door, and she didn't answer. Her door was unlocked, so I went inside. She wasn't there."

Ben Barten came quickly down the stairs, his face worried and desperate.

"She's nowhere to be found, Reverend," he concluded. "I searched everywhere upstairs."

"Every room?"

"Well, not every room, but anywhere she'd likely be."

"A thorough search must be conducted. Let's split up in twos and search every room, every closet. Jessica, we need flashlights, oil lamps, candles, whatever."

Jessica nodded, and produced another flashlight, and two oil lamps from a closet behind the front desk. Each pair of investigators set off in the darkness. The temperature within the Lodge was dropping noticeably, as the power had now been off for a long time.

Harvey held his watch by the fire so he could read it. It read 4:30 A.M. He shook his head in realization of how long he had been without sleep. He turned to face the group, now reassembled by the fire. Most looked as though they had not slept either. A complete search of the Lodge had been made. No trace of Barten's girlfriend had been found. She had simply disappeared.

"Perhaps she tried to escape the Lodge," said Helen.

A furious Ben Barten rose to his feet. "And just what are you suggesting, Miss Roma?"

"I'm suggesting nothing," she replied. "All I am pointing out is that we've had two murders and another attempted one. And now, Julie has gone."

"No one in their right mind would attempt to get through this storm on foot," said Harvey. "I'm more inclined at this point to fear for Julie's life, as a yet-undiscovered victim."

"But why, Reverend?" asked Barten. "Why Julie? What could she possibly have done?"

"That, Mr. Barten, is a good question. I have come to realize that many of us here had a reason to wish that the sale of the Lodge not take place. Whether some of those reasons are worth killing for is debatable. But someone capable of murder is unlikely to be an individual ruled by rationality. But although motives for Galen's death exist, the link to Lisa Aames, and now possibly to Julie, escape me. I'm sorry to have to have go into this, but it is necessary to ascertain each person's movements during the last two hours."

"Two hours?" said Helen. "Why two?"

"Sarah and I were doing some . . . investigating downstairs."

Mayor Halon stood up suddenly. "Downstairs?"

"Yes, Mayor," replied Harvey. "Is that a problem?"

The mayor reseated himself, "Well, no, of course not. But was it wise to be fumbling around late at night under our current circumstances?"

"Probably not, Mayor, but I had to check on some things."

"What did you find?" asked Mast.

"Well, at this point, I prefer to keep that to myself. What I am now concerned about is what happened to us."

"And what was that?" asked Barten.

"We were examining the body of the second victim, in the freezer. While we were in there, someone came in behind us and locked us in."

"That's horrible!" said Helen, looking shocked. "Why would someone want to do that?"

"Why indeed, Miss Roma?" he replied. "Clearly there is something down there that someone does not want us to find."

"Well, we were all in our rooms, Reverend," offered Jim Mast.

"Were you?" questioned Harvey. "I saw Jessica and Floyd down here within minutes of the event. Any of you could have been down here as well, hiding in the shadows. Do any of you have witnesses to confirm your presence in your rooms?"

"Well, Jessica found each of us locked in our rooms," said the mayor.

"Given the time available, Jessica," continued Harvey, "could anyone have managed to get up to their room from the basement without any of us seeing them?"

Jessica put down her coffee cup. "Anyone could have, Reverend. There is a fire escape stairway on that side of the Lodge leading upstairs."

"And while we were locked in the freezer they could have gone up that way without us seeing them," said Harvey.

"If they were fast about it, and managed to get out there before I came down."

''Assuming it wasn't you, Jessica,'' accused Helen.

''Helen, I swear, I had only just come down to investigate the shot I heard!''

''Now ladies,'' said Harvey, ''let's not turn on each other, and make random accusations. It's clear that anyone here could have done it.''

''What shot are you talking about, Jessica?'' said the mayor.

''Reverend Ashe used his pistol to shoot the lock off of the freezer door,'' explained Jessica.

''Yes, that's right,'' agreed Harvey. ''Or else we'd still be in there, suffocating.''

''And freezing,'' added Sarah.

''Reverend Ashe.'' cried Helen, again in tears. ''What is going on here? When will it all stop?''

''There is an awful lot going on here,'' said Harvey. ''More than is being said, I'm afraid.''

''What do you mean?'' asked Halon.

Harvey sat down on the hearth next to the fire. Scott Grey walked over and stood in front of Harvey.

''Reverend Ashe,'' Grey said, ''I think this whole thing is getting to you. Perhaps you should give up this futile investigation and wait for the police like we should have to begin with. Maybe no one else will get hurt.''

''What makes you think the rest of us want the investigation stopped?'' demanded Jessica.

''I only know what I want! That's all I care about.

Getting out of here alive. Everybody else seems to want to play detective and get us all killed!''

''That's enough, both of you!'' ordered Harvey with a sudden forcefulness as he stood. ''This is solving nothing. Now just sit down and relax. The killer would love nothing more than to see us all turn on one another and save him the trouble.''

With his stare, Harvey caused Grey to back down, and go to his seat. Harvey returned to his seat by the fire.

''I just need to think for a little while, and try to put things together.''

Chapter Nine

Sarah's eyes glinted from the gently flickering flame of the oil lamp on the desk. She and Harvey had felt the need to get alone to discuss their predicament. She could hear that the wind had begun to subside. Perhaps the blizzard was finally tapering off.

"Harvey," Sarah began, "you look very tired. You need rest, and you can't take this for much longer without becoming exhausted. You're not as young as you once were, you know."

"If only I could rest, dear. Until this is over, I just can't."

"Well, what are your thoughts about all this? Any conclusions? Any theories? I for one am concerned about Jessica Barrow."

"As am I. As far as motive, it has become clear to me that she has the most to gain."

"Really? What leads you to that?" said Sarah, puzzled.

"Something I've yet to have the opportunity to let you in on, dear, but very important. As you recall, we determined from the sales contract of the Lodge that in the event that Mr. Galen died intestate, and without natural heir, ownership reverts to the estate of the original owner."

"Jordan Clarckston?"

"Yes. I knew that I remembered seeing that name somewhere else, but couldn't quite place it. I went to great pains to find out who might be related to the Clarckstons. As it turns out, the one I did not ask was the one. Jessica Barrow."

"How did you find out?"

Harvey reached for a file folder on the desk and handed it to Sarah.

"Only a little while ago, Floyd told me that Jessica mentioned the old owner's name to him. He remembered that I had been inquiring about who knew of the family, and thought I should know that Jessica had dropped the name quite on her own. That's when it came to me where else I had seen the name. In Jessica's personnel file. In some of the older paperwork, you see that Barrow is her maiden name, and that she was once married."

"To a Clarckston?"

"To Jordan Clarckston himself."

"If so, what is she doing working here, with Galen?"

Harvey returned the file to the desk drawer. "I don't know the answer to that. I've yet to have the chance to question her about it. But clearly if John Galen had no will, then Jessica would become the owner if he died. She has an obvious interest in seeing that the sale of the Lodge not happen. And, she spent most of the time in question running back and forth between the dining room and the kitchen. She could very easily have picked up some object in the kitchen and gone outside, and killed Galen without anyone else noticing her absence. No one was really paying attention to anyone else's movements, not expecting a murder."

Sarah's eyes widened as she followed Harvey's train of thought.

"And Harvey," she added, "remember who we first saw when we escaped from the freezer?"

"Jessica. And until last night, she also had the pass-keys to the rooms, which would have enabled her to enter Lisa Aames's room."

"But why? What's the motive there?"

"Simply to cover up tracks. As I said to begin with, Lisa knew or discovered something that cost her her life."

"If so, then why did Jessica enlist your help? She has been a vocal supporter of your investigation all along, even over the objections of the others."

Harvey tugged nervously at his mustache. "Though it damages my ego somewhat, I must admit that getting an aging ex-police officer-turned preacher to muck the case up would no doubt increase her chances of getting away with it. What better way of diverting suspicion than initiating the effort to solve the crime?"

"True, very true," Sarah agreed with a sigh. "So is that your official verdict?"

Harvey stood up and looked out the window. The first gray signs of dawn were fighting through the storm.

"In many ways it makes sense. But there are other considerations that warrant serious thought. Almost everyone had reason or at least opportunity."

"Like Jessica, Floyd had plenty of time to get outside to do the deed. But why would he?"

"He certainly would be harmed if the Lodge went out of business. You see, after close examination of information in his file, I determined that the reason he works here is because he has little other choice. Floyd was the head chef at a four-star restaurant in Philadelphia. This is where he met John Galen, who is from the same area. There was a great scandal in that establishment regarding coverups of unexplained sicknesses and deaths of patrons. Accusations of unsanitary conditions and food poisoning hit the papers, and the place was soon out of business. The owners did time for the coverup. From what I read in the newspaper clipping regarding his testimony, Floyd evidently took the fall for someone else. Needless to say, although he was never charged, he could never work in that state again. John Galen gave him this job. As a matter of fact, I wouldn't be surprised if there might have been some blackmail going on. Galen's bank book showed numerous cash payments from unexplained sources.''

''Is Floyd capable of killing on account of this?''

''I doubt he would just over his job. But if Galen was blackmailing him, then perhaps. However, when I think about the mysterious cash payments, I keep going back to Mayor Halon and his little shadow, Jim Mast.''

''The gambling paraphernalia?''

''Yes. Clearly there is an illegal gambling operation going on down there, and John Galen was in on it. The mayor kept talking about how he loved to entertain his business associates here, and how he would try to attract business to the town. A little fun at an illegal casino would do the trick. The sale of the Lodge would end all that.''

''But he could easily relocate the games. Why kill Galen?''

''Since delving in to all this, I'm no longer convinced of Galen's character. I wouldn't be surprised if Halon was worried about being exposed by Galen. This would ruin him. Definitely a motive for murder. And during the time of the killing, the mayor went upstairs for some reason. We already know about the fire escape that would give him quick access to Galen's location at the woodshed. For that matter, Jim Mast went out the front door at the same time. He said it was to smoke a cigarette. That has bothered me ever since he said it. I realize what an addiction tobacco is, but would someone really go outside into a blizzard and fifty-mile-an-hour winds to satisfy his habit? It seems unlikely to me. And given the time, Mast could have run around the corner of the building and killed Galen, or helped the mayor do it.''

''So where does that leave us?''

Harvey turned back toward the desk, and reached into his pocket.

''And then there's this. . . .'' Harvey held forth a diamond ring.

Sarah stood up and took the ring, examining it closely.

''Why, this is Helen Roma's engagement ring. Did you get this from her room?''

Harvey shook his head. ''No, dear, I pulled it from John Galen's desk drawer.''

''But Helen told us she took it off because of the grief she was feeling.''

''Well, she took it off all right, but not when she said she did. Evidently, she either gave it back to him . . .''

''Or he demanded it back.''

''Yes, and I heard them having an argument just before dinner.''

Sarah handed the ring back to Harvey, who replaced it in his pocket. "And she was very quiet during dinner."

"Somewhat uncharacteristic for her, I gather," noted Harvey.

Sarah nodded. "So perhaps something happened between them."

Harvey dropped back in his chair. "It leads nowhere. She has nothing to gain and everything to lose by killing him. If she can manage to reconcile and marry John, she'd be a rich woman, if the sale of the Lodge goes as planned. As it is now, she has nothing. Besides, I saw her go into Galen's office to take that phone call during that time with my own eyes."

"I wonder who called her. Did you ask her?"

"No. At the time I didn't think it to be important. Knowing who called her, and verifying that with the other party, would only serve to solidify her alibi. Once the phones are up, we can do that, of course, but it still doesn't advance the case."

"Except to eliminate someone."

"True again. But I'm more concerned with everyone's safety at this point. Revealing the culprit is paramount."

Sarah rubbed her neck, as she closed her eyes in thought.

"Scott Grey?" she asked.

"He had the chance. He was standing out in the sunroom. He could have gone out the door and down the steps and killed him. But why? Galen's death virtually ends his real estate deal, from which he has the potential of making big money.''

''Unless he is also related to the Clarckstons,'' said Sarah.

''Go on . . .'' Harvey prompted.

''Well, let's just say he's a nephew, or an in-law. Why pay all the money to own the property when you can just kill Galen and inherit it for nothing?''

''Does anything lead you to believe he is related?''

''Nothing concrete. It just seems strange that he would come all the way out here from Las Vegas, passing thousands of areas just as suitable for development, and try to buy this out-of-the-way place. Unless he had some personal interest or knowledge of the place.''

Harvey nodded. ''It's possible, but what about Jessica? We know she's related.''

''They could be in it together.''

''Yes, that's true, of course, but it's all so hypothetical. We really can't arrive at conclusive facts isolated from the world like this. We can't even be sure of who all these people are. I'm beginning to wonder about myself.''

Sarah picked up a pencil and began doodling on the desk blotter as they both thought silently.

''We haven't mentioned Ben or Julie,'' she said.

''I never saw them come out of the back dining

room until later. There's no way out of there that leads outside.''

''They did stay in there talking quite a bit.''

''And Barten gains nothing by killing Galen, except losing a client.''

Sarah took Harvey's rough hand, and stroked it gently, trying to relax him.

''Harvey, what do you think happened to Julie?''

Harvey shook his head. ''I don't think—''

Harvey was interrupted by the phone suddenly ringing. The sound startled them, causing Sarah to jump slightly.

''The phone?'' said Sarah.

''Maybe it's working again,'' said Harvey as he picked up the receiver. ''Hello . . .''

Harvey's eyes widened as he listened.

''Reverend Ashe,'' came Jessica's voice from the receiver, ''this is Jessica. I think you'd better come up to the third floor, to Julie's room. . . .''

''Jessica . . . I thought the phones were out.''

''They still serve as intercoms, even if the lines are down. They have a battery backup even in the event of a power outage. But that's beside the point—we've found Julie.''

''And . . .''

''I think you'd better come up here, to room 325.''

''We'll be right there.''

Harvey hung up the phone.

"What is it, Harvey?" Sarah asked as they rose and headed for the door.

"I think your question about Julie is about to be answered."

Sarah grabbed the lamp at the last moment, as Harvey led her by the other hand upstairs. Their rapid footsteps on the hardwood stairs reverberated loudly as they rushed. Harvey could feel his heart pounding as he approached the third-floor landing. Sarah was still right behind him, keeping up with every step.

The remainder of the group had already assembled at the doorway of Julie's room. Helen Roma held her hand over her mouth, attempting to hide the quivering of her lower lip. Harvey pushed through the group and made his way into the room. Jessica and Ben Barten were outside on the balcony, leaning over the edge. Harvey rushed to join them.

"Jessica, Mr. Barten . . ."

"Reverend!" cried Jessica. "It's Julie!"

"She's dead, Reverend Ashe!" yelled Barten.

Harvey looked over the side and saw Julie hanging by the neck, from the belt of a bathrobe. She swung in the wind, banging against the side of the building. The beginnings of sunlight were breaking through the cloud cover, and the ice crystals forming on her body were glistening like tiny lights.

Harvey and Ben worked together to pull her body over the railing and back into the room, where she was laid carefully on the bed. Harvey's face was tightened with anger. He slowly gazed at each face in the room, one at a time. Each person cringed as Harvey's glare met them.

Chapter Ten

Since daylight had come, and the storm winds subsided, Floyd Helton had managed to get to the outside storage shed. It was there among the garden tools, lawn mowers, and other landscaping equipment that he had found extra gasoline. With this he was able to start the emergency generator and restore limited power to the Lodge. Heating, lighting, and, fortunately, cooking, were again possible.

Harvey Ashe stood solemnly in the sunroom portion of the dining hall. He gazed vacantly across the snow-covered mountainscape before him. Snowdrifts had accumulated below the sunroom level, almost covering the basement area. The Lodge overlooked a great valley, now appearing like a monstrous white river spilling out into the flatland beyond.

154

He sensed quiet footsteps approaching from behind.

"Now that the storm has passed I imagine that the phone lines will be up soon," Jessica theorized. "Maybe help won't be far behind. This will all be over soon."

"Miss Barrow," said Harvey dourly, "why did you not tell me that you are to inherit the Briar Ridge Lodge now that John Galen is dead? And that you were married to the previous owner?"

Harvey turned as he hurled the question, as if to impart momentum to it. His eyes were no longer gentle.

"Reverend, um . . ." Jessica was visibly stunned. "Oh, my. . . ."

"That is not an answer, Miss Barrow."

"Reverend, I know how it must look to you."

"I sincerely doubt you do."

"Well, I did not kill John. He was my friend. He was good to me. I did not think that the facts of my marriage to Jordan were relevant."

Harvey motioned for her to sit down at the table. As she sat down, he also pulled up a chair.

"In situations such as this, it is never wise to withhold any information. You must allow investigators to determine what is pertinent, and what is not. Silence on these issues only serves to bring suspicion. Surely, you must have known that when the storm was over, and legal proceedings began, it would all come out."

"Yes, of course, I knew that. But again, I didn't want to alarm anyone."

"But since you have been discovered anyway, you have alarmed me. Perhaps the complete truth is in order."

Jessica toyed with a napkin on the table.

"Jordan and I were very happy. He was fairly wealthy, at least from my standpoint. But he lost a lot of money in bad investments. He sold this Lodge as a desperate measure to generate cash flow. Not long after he died. Quite typical of the intense, high-risk business type—he suffered a heart attack. Died instantly while on the phone in his office. When all was said and done, all the debts paid, virtually nothing was left. John gave me this job, I guess out of pity. He knew the family, you see. He felt sorry for me. I swallowed my pride and took the job. I had no other choice."

"But you were aware of the provisions of the contract, that you would inherit the place if John died intestate?"

"Yes, Jordan had told me he put such a stipulation in the contract. To tell you the truth, I didn't really think I would end up with it. I assumed that what almost did happen would happen. John would get married, and make a will favoring his family, or that he would just sell it. And I would get nothing . . . again."

Harvey was looking directly into her tired eyes.

"Jessica, I'm truly sorry for what you've been

through. But you must realize that nothing you have said changes your situation.''

''What do you mean?''

''I've already resigned myself to the fact that you had the opportunity to kill him. And I've suspected a motive. You've just now confirmed the motive. In fact, you're the only one here with a clear motive.''

''Is that an official accusation? Are you placing me under arrest, being a deputy and all? Don't you have to read me my rights or something?''

''No, Jessica, I am not. But if you're innocent, give me a reason to believe otherwise.''

''What about Lisa Aames?''

''Until last night, you had the passkeys. Entering her room and switching her medication would be no trouble at all. And you were the one who found Julie.''

''But why would I kill either of them?''

''Perhaps Lisa knew about the sales contract. Perhaps she knew you would inherit. Perhaps in a frantic panic, you thought she was the only one who could endanger you until you could escape. At this point, I must confess I can't imagine a motive for killing Julie. But where one exists, it will surface.''

''Reverend Ashe, you're jumping to conclusions. You have no basis or proof for what you're saying.''

''Then help me. All that you say in your defense can be explained; you are correct. I want to believe you. But you see, I have already caught you in a lie.''

"But I didn't lie about Jordan, I just didn't mention it."

"I don't mean that. I mean about the wood."

Jessica was puzzled.

"What?"

"You see, John was sent out into the storm to get wood from the woodshed. But after we had discovered his murder, and came back inside, I noticed that the wood box beside the fireplace was full. So why did you send John Galen out into the storm? I heard you tell him myself."

Jessica stood suddenly, confusion on her face.

"But it wasn't me."

Harvey stood up next to her.

"But I heard you."

"I know that I said it to him. But it wasn't my idea. I mean I was busy working in the kitchen. Someone else yelled it out, that John needed to go get firewood. I didn't even bother to check the wood box myself. It was so hectic and I was upset about the sale of the Lodge, and all . . . I just don't really remember."

"Remember what?"

"Who it was that mentioned to me to send John out."

Harvey took her arm gently, and turned Jessica toward him.

"Jessica, this is very important. You must remember who it was."

Jessica seemed to strain over her memories, her eyes

narrowed to slits. Then she opened them wide, and turned and looked back into the main dining room, where the rest of the group was still sitting. Harvey nodded as he saw the one Jessica was peering toward.

"Are you positive?" he asked as she turned back toward him.

"I'm certain."

"And now the rest of it makes sense," Harvey seemed to say to himself. "Jessica, your freedom may depend on this. As you said yourself, we require proof. This is what I need you to do. . . ."

The entire group was assembled in the reserved dining room, the same room in which John Galen had eaten his last meal only two nights before. All were seated except Harvey Ashe, who stood at the head of the table.

"Now that the storm has let up," he began, "we are sure the police will be here soon. Sheriff Randall was, as you recall, made aware of our situation before the phones went out. We will no doubt be a priority as soon as travel is possible. I have come to realize that before that time—that is, when each of us can leave—we must come to a conclusion about this case."

"Have you reached a solution, Reverend?" asked a beleaguered Helen Roma.

"Yes, I believe I have. You see, although John Galen owned the Lodge, he didn't run it, not really.

Jessica Barrow is the real workhorse in this place. And believe me, nothing goes unnoticed by her. Even things that are supposed to be big secrets. You see, Jessica remembers who called to her through the confusion of the other night, to send John Galen outside to get firewood, even though the wood box was quite full. And she knows a few other things as well . . .''

''What do you mean?'' asked Floyd.

''I think you know, sir.''

At that cue, Jessica reached into her jacket pocket and produced a single blue poker chip. She threw it into the center of the table as if it were a gruesome wager. Mayor Halon swallowed hard. Jessica again reached into her pocket, and produced a playing card. It was the king of diamonds. She tossed it to the table next to the poker chip.

''What's your point, Ashe?'' demanded a belligerent Jim Mast.

''I think you know very well, Mr. Mast. You and the mayor have been carrying on an illegal gambling operation in the Lodge for years. As I understand it, you've both skimmed quite a tidy sum off the top. You stand to lose a lot if the Lodge is sold, and your little game is put to an end.''

''Ashe,'' said the mayor, ''you don't know what you're saying. One poker chip and a playing card could come from anywhere.''

''Yes, they could,'' said Jessica, ''but in fact they

came from the cabinet downstairs, with all the other casino equipment.''

Helen Roma erupted in tears. ''I can't stand it anymore. When will all this end? Why would they do this?''

Helen started coughing and choking as she sobbed. Harvey nodded to Sarah, who embraced her comfortingly.

''I'm so sorry,'' Helen apologized. ''I think I need a glass of water.''

Sarah helped her stand up, as they were excused to the kitchen.

''You see, Ashe,'' warned Mast, ''all this is upsetting her terribly!''

''Yes, I thought it might. Nonetheless, this has to come to an end.''

''You've gone too far. Maybe you should just abandon all this, and wait for the real police like we said all along.''

''I'm sure that's just what you'd like, Mr. Mast. But I'm afraid it's too late for that.''

''What possible reason would we have for conspiring to kill John Galen?'' said the mayor.

''I've already told you. Your game was up, and I think that Galen was blackmailing you on top of it. Your reelection campaign is only months away. I'm sure your opponent would love to find out about all this. And I've already established that both you and

Mast could have had the time to go outside and kill him.''

''It'll never stick, Reverend,'' taunted the Mayor, ''any more than any of your pathetic sermons.''

''Mayor Halon,'' said Ben Barten, ''how could you say such a thing? Is he telling the truth about all this?''

The mayor and Jim Mast were both silent.

''Harvey!'' called Sarah from the kitchen.

Harvey came to the door and met Sarah running from the lobby.

''What is it, dear?''

''It's Helen,'' informed Sarah. ''She's completely beside herself with fear. She said she knew she'd be next; she had to get away.''

Everyone was now looking at Mayor Halon, not pleasantly.

''Mr. Barten, Mr. Grey, if you would see to it that the Honorable Mr. Mayor and Mr. Mast are confined to their rooms until the police arrive.''

''Harvey, where are you going?'' asked Sarah.

''I'm going to find Helen. It was my dramatics that upset her and sent her out into the snow.''

''But where could she go? There's not another house for miles,'' said Sarah.

''She might be able to reach the Craft Village, down the hill,'' said Jessica. ''It's closed up now, but she might try to hide there, if she's afraid.''

''Harvey, you don't have to do this,'' said Sarah.

"My dear," replied Harvey, "you know very well that I do."

Sarah nodded with resignation. Harvey picked up his coat, which he had earlier left in the lobby, and headed out the front door into the blinding snow.

Chapter Eleven

It was difficult for Harvey to walk in the snow, still harder when he tried to run. The depth of the snow was above his knees, and the intense cold was soon penetrating his shoes. Though the wind had subsided, the air was still dangerously cold. His face felt as though it were being bitten by the atmosphere itself. The brightness of the sun reflecting off of the pure white snow caused him to squint. He thought it was going to be easy to follow Helen's tracks, but in the glare he had to squint so as not to be blinded. Seeing anything other than the monotonous whiteness was difficult.

As he approached what he thought was the road, he stopped to take stock of his position. He knew the road approaching the Lodge wound its way up the side of the mountain. The snowdrifts obscured the edge, so he had to be careful. He didn't want to step off the edge and tumble down the mountain trying to catch an hysterical Helen Roma. He thought he could distinguish tracks in the snow ahead, now that some of the evergreens blocked the sunshine. At least Helen had not plunged off the mountainside yet. He continued down the road. His feet were already numb. If he didn't get out of this and into warm shelter soon, he would succumb to frostbite. This painful condition he had suffered before, and he did not wish to go through it again, though Helen's survival depended on the risk.

It seemed an eternity when Harvey finally reached the lofty but empty oak that signaled the fork in the road. To the right was the main highway, though it scarcely appeared as such now. To his left was a small drive leading to the very popular, yet now deserted, Craft Village. Slowly, he trudged toward the left.

The relentless cold seemed to be permeating his brain. His thoughts were disjointed, random. Perhaps this was the beginnings of hypothermia, or just his own physical exhaustion. As he looked upward through the trees, he could see the back of the Lodge hanging off of the side of the peak of Briar Ridge Mountain. It looked like a frosting-covered ornament atop a monstrous vanilla-iced cake.

He could now see split-rail fenceposts poking out of snowdrifts on each side of the path. This indicated the outskirts of the small Craft Village. As he rounded the corner, he saw the first building.

The Village was essentially one narrow street, extending about the length of a city block. Lining each side of the street were small rustic shops with plank sidewalks. It almost resembled a town of the Old West in its design, though now it appeared to be a ghost town. At the other end of the street was another split-rail fence marking the end of the road. He knew there to be a small picnic area beyond, and then more fence to prevent careless tourists from plunging off the side of the mountain into the river-gouged valley below.

Harvey walked slowly down the middle of the road, looking for signs that Helen had come this way. All the buildings were locked, but windows could be broken.

Three doors down and to the right, Harvey could see footprints in the snow on the walk in the front of one of the shops. The snow was shallower there, the walk being sheltered somewhat by the overhang of the building. A gentle breeze was now blowing from the valley, and Harvey could hear the squeaking of the store sign swinging in the moving air. The sign read *Mountain Creations*, and the lettering was made to look like branches and twigs. Harvey knew this store to be run by an elderly man living on the other side of the mountain. His name was Esmer Collins, and he was skilled in woodcarving, and sold novelty items. He was very good at his craft, but a little strange.

When Harvey was helping Sarah at her shop across the street during the busy season, Esmer would always corner him and ramble on about odd things that happened in the woods at night, or about the strange woman he knew who lived across the valley and practiced witchcraft. Harvey shuddered more from thinking of Esmer than from the cold.

He approached the front door of the shop, and noted it was still locked, and all looked secure. He looked down at the footprints, and saw them continue around the corner of the building. He followed them down the narrow alley between the two shops, and to the back door. He saw more footprints on the back stoop. He looked up to see a couple of broken windowpanes in the back door.

Cautiously, Harvey stepped onto the stoop, and cupped his hands around his eyes as he peered into the back of the store. It was too dark to see anything. He reached for the doorknob. It was as cold as a dead man's hand as he turned it. It was unlocked, and he slowly pulled the door open. The hinges creaked as the door swung open.

"Helen?" he called into the dark back room. "Helen, are you in here?"

He stepped into the room, and pulled the door closed behind him.

"Helen, we'll both freeze to death if we don't get back to the Lodge . . . please, show yourself."

Harvey groped his way toward the lighter front

room. As he stepped across the threshold, he heard the rapid swishing of air, and a sudden piercing, throbbing pain in the back of his head. His field of vision seemed to black out for a moment, but he did not completely lose consciousness. The blow caused him to stagger forward, and he kept himself from hitting the floor only by leaning against a counter display full of delicate wood carvings. As he pushed against the counter, it shook, and several of the creations toppled and fell to the floor. They seemed to fall in slow motion to Harvey, as he struggled to recover his senses.

Harvey's ears were ringing, so he couldn't really hear the approach, but he could feel the floor vibrating with footsteps. He gathered all his strength to pull himself to the other side of the counter, and to look up at his attacker.

''Helen!'' he said, holding up his hand as if to stay another assault. ''Please . . . I am not your enemy.''

Helen's eyes were wildly gleaming in the sunlight beaming through the front windows. They were not eyes of fear, but of anger. In his stunned condition, they were unnerving to Harvey, but he refused to show it. He was beginning to regain his composure now, but he still grasped the edge of the counter for support.

''Why did you run, Helen?'' Harvey said.

''I had to run, I had to get away!''

''Sarah . . . she gave you the ring back, didn't she?'' he said, nodding toward her left hand. The diamond engagement ring sparkled in the light. Helen briefly looked at the ring, then back at Harvey.

''I know he hurt you, Helen,'' Harvey continued. ''I know that he hurt you badly . . . casting you aside on the very eve of your new, wealthy life together. I know how hard it must have been to watch him flirting with his new plaything, right under your nose, a young, vibrant girl named Julie.''

Harvey could sense her mental defenses strengthening as her grip on the walking stick she wielded tightened.

''Reverend Ashe,'' she protested vehemently, ''I heard you revealing all that about the mayor and Jim Mast. I ran because I was frightened of them, of what they might do.''

''Then why attack me, Helen? You've already tried to kill Sarah and me once, by locking us in the freezer. You killed Lisa Aames because she was the only one who knew your alibi was faked. You see, I know it was you who told Jessica to send John Galen out to get wood, even thought the wood box was full. You didn't think anyone would notice. You killed Julie just out of spite, for taking him away from you. Like I said, I am not the enemy, Miss Roma, you are.''

Helen held her weapon high as she shuffled sideways toward the front door.

She muttered an expletive. ''I never imagined I'd get stranded in this storm with you people!'' Her shoulders twitched with rage as she murmured to herself, "It should have been so easy. . . ."

Harvey calmly asked, "Why Lisa? Why did you have to involve her?"

Helen smirked. "She was an easy mark. She thought I was her friend. We laughed over the little joke we would play to get me out of the dinner. By the time I had switched her glucagon for the insulin, she was already so shaky from the sweets I'd tempted her with all day, she wasn't able to think straight."

Her tone was detached and cruel.

"You're just lucky she didn't pass into a coma before she made your phone call," said Harvey coolly.

"I'm used to taking risks with people I want out of the way . . . Reverend." She raised the stick again. Harvey wondered how many others had gotten in her way in the past.

"Helen," Harvey said as he matched her moves, "there's no sense in running now. There's no place left to run. You can't survive out there for very long. There's not another house for miles. Just put that down, and let's get back to the Lodge. A voluntary surrender is always—"

Harvey's plea was interrupted as Helen swung the stick toward his head. He ducked, and it missed him. It crashed into shelving behind the cash register. When Harvey looked up, the door was open, and Helen was gone. Harvey could feel the relative warmth of the shop being sucked out into the open air. He followed her out into the street.

He looked to the right, and saw Helen running toward the picnic area, stumbling occasionally in the deep snow.

"Helen!" he called. But she ignored him, and continued toward the woods.

Harvey stepped gingerly off of the frozen walkway, and set off toward Helen. He momentarily lost sight of her behind a row of now-empty freestanding booths. Harvey thought that Helen must be insane to attempt this escape. There was nowhere for her to run, and no way to evade eventual justice. Even if she survived the elements long enough to get off the mountain, this community was too small for her to hide. Running murderers, however, did not always think logically.

Harvey carefully and slowly crept behind the first booth, expecting Helen to be there to strike at him again. As he looked down the pathway behind the booths, he saw nothing. Just to his left, the split-rail fence on the edge of the hill stretched ahead of him. The snow-laden evergreens hung low over the railing, and he could see no farther than twelve feet ahead. He held on to the fence and moved forward, as quietly as possible.

He could not see her, but he felt the fence shake and vibrate. He surmised that Helen was climbing over the fence. He quickened his pace through the drooping tree limbs.

Then, he heard the gentle but powerful sound of shifting snow, and Helen's muffled gasp. Quickly he arrived at the spot. The top rail had been knocked out of its place by Helen's climbing. Apparently, Helen had stepped out onto what appeared to be solid ground. Instead, it was a massive snowdrift with no foundation. She immediately lost her footing and tumbled down the side of the hill. Harvey stepped across what was left of that section of the fence, holding on to the post for safety. He looked down the hill to see Helen's body deposited at the bottom. The drop had not been that far, but judging by the skewed position of her head, Helen must have tumbled headfirst, and broken her delicate neck. She did not move, and the gentle breeze was blowing snowflakes into her hair, and onto her pale, surprised face. Harvey released the deep breath he had been holding.

Chapter Twelve

The snowplow was making its way back down the driveway of the Briar Ridge Lodge, toward the main highway. In the partially cleared parking lot were several police cruisers, including Sheriff Randall's car, and two ambulances. There was a flurry of activity as the EMTs wheeled covered bodies from the Lodge.

The front door swung open, and three handcuffed figures emerged, led by police officers. The officers escorted Mayor Halon, Jim Mast, and Floyd Helton into separate cars. Local newspaper and television reporters were recording the event with sadistic glee.

"Three murders *and* an illegal gambling ring broken up in one weekend," mused Sheriff Randall. "Not bad for a city-born preacher!"

173

Harvey laughed as he sat down on the sofa in the dining room, handing a fresh cup of coffee to Sarah.

"I think your job is secure, Sheriff," assured Harvey.

"That's the last of them," a relieved Jessica Barrow said as she returned from the front desk. "Everyone's checked out except you two. They were most eager to get out of here."

"And so are we," said Sarah, nudging Harvey's elbow. "I want to get out of here as soon as possible. Let's get upstairs and get packed."

"Just a minute, Reverend," insisted Jessica. "You've got to clear up a few things. I know that I was able to remember that Helen was the one who told me to send John out to get the wood, but how did she manage it? You said yourself that you saw her on the phone during that time."

"I'd like you to spell it out for me, too, Reverend," said Randall. "For my report, you know."

Harvey took another sip of coffee.

"I actually never saw her on the phone. You see, that whole phone call business bugged me from the beginning. I saw her go into the office, but the door was closed. I was trying to make a call myself to my assistant pastor. I had to wait, because both lines were busy. I knew that Helen was on the phone, but I couldn't imagine who else would be tying up the line. It wasn't until Jessica called me this morning from upstairs using the intercom function that I realized that whoever called Helen was calling from inside the Lodge, at another extension.''

''The only other extensions that don't go through the switchboard are the ones at the end of each hallway of each floor,'' said Jessica.

''Yes, and there's one right outside Lisa Aames's room. You see, when Lisa came upstairs the other night, I overheard her telling someone that she 'wouldn't forget,' and mentioned the time, eight o'clock. That was the precise time Helen got the phone call.''

''So Helen had convinced Lisa to call her at that time to invent an alibi? Why would Lisa do it?'' asked Jessica.

''We'll never know, of course, but I expect she probably just told her she wanted a graceful way of getting out of the dinner party. Maybe she told Lisa about John breaking up with her. I doubt Lisa had any idea she was helping Helen carry out a murder.''

''But how did she do it?'' asked Randall, taking notes.

''While secure in the assumption that we all knew she was in the office, on the phone, she sneaked out the other door, leading into the kitchen. She followed John while no one was in the kitchen, and killed him.''

''With what?'' asked Randall.

''There are some shelves behind Galen's desk. They're all covered with dust. I don't suppose that he was a very tidy man. But I noticed that there were patterns in the dust where objects had been, and recently moved, since the last dusting. It was obvious that someone had taken everything off the shelf very recently. One of those metal shelf brackets would make quite a formidable weapon if used with sufficient force. And I found out how hard that woman can swing!''

Harvey rubbed the knot on the back of his head.

''I expect, Sheriff,'' he continued, ''that if forensics examines those brackets, they will find microscopic remnants of blood from John Galen's head. The objects are consistent with the wound.''

Jessica was shaking her head, still in disbelief. ''I still can't believe she would be so violent. She seemed like such a gentle lady.''

''She fooled more than you,'' said Harvey. ''Sheriff, I suspect that if you investigate her past, you will likely uncover other unsolved deaths. She intimated earlier successes with those who got in her way. In Galen's defense, I doubt he really had any idea just what kind of woman he had hooked up with. He had only known her for a few years, and knew nothing about her background. If she had lived, Sheriff, I'm sure a psychological profile would have indicated a very unbalanced mind. She always seemed very close to the edge, you know. All weekend long she appeared nearly hysterical, on the verge of a breakdown. We all thought it was grief over losing John, coupled with fear for her own life at the hands of an unknown killer.

But instead, it was a constant state of jealous rage. Down in the shop, earlier, I saw it in her eyes. She would have killed me as she tried to last night . . . simply because she feared discovery. I had dared to foil her plan. Julie, on the other hand, had done nothing to her. She was simply the unfortunate object of John Galen's new attentions. As the fabled 'other woman,' she suffered the most violent of all the deaths.''

''Pretty good detective work, Reverend,'' complimented Randall.

Harvey shook his head. ''Not really. I should have seen the obvious much sooner. Perhaps Julie would have lived, at least. You see, I was confused because of the mayor's distractions. I knew that he and Mast were up to something. They were acting too suspicious. But I just couldn't see a motive for murder.''

''But what about the blackmail you mentioned?'' asked Jessica.

''I made that up. The cash payments were probably his cut of the gambling money, as payment for using the Lodge as a casino. I was just trying to make them look guilty to keep from tipping my hand to Helen. Sarah giving her back the ring we found in Galen's desk was what really set her off, though. It was then she realized that we knew about their breakup. So she ran. Foolishly, as there was nowhere for her to go.''

''I think she knew she wouldn't survive,'' said Sarah. ''When she ran I don't think it was escape she was looking for, but release. She hadn't counted on being confined here for three days after the murder. It was getting to her. I think she just wanted to get out and die alone. But that's just an opinion.''

'' 'She openeth her mouth with wisdom . . .' '' quoted Harvey with a tired smile. ''Far be it from me to dispute your opinions, dear.''

''Perhaps I will forgive you, Reverend,'' said Jessica slyly, ''for suspecting me.''

''I never really suspected you, Jessica,'' admitted Harvey. ''But you were the only one with a clear motive at the time. I knew that confronting you with the accusation would cause you to act against me if you were guilty. If you weren't, then I knew you'd add vital information in trying to clear yourself. Which is exactly what you did by fingering the one who set the whole thing in motion.''

Sarah patted Harvey's knee. ''Harvey, dear, we've got to go. Your precious children are no doubt anxious to see you.''

Harvey smiled. ''Oh yes, I'm looking forward to seeing Ulysses and Muffin. I'm sure they missed me tremendously.''

''Harvey, I was talking about Laura, your real daughter. I just talked to her on the phone, and she was worried sick. They want us to get there as soon as we can. She'll fix dinner.''

Harvey cocked his head in thought. ''What is she fixing?''

Sarah gave Harvey a playful slap on the arm. ''What difference does that make?''

''Well, I just thought that if she was making that chocolate fudge cake . . .''

''I'm sure that if you ask her, she'll put one together tonight, if she hasn't already.''

Harvey stood up. ''Let's go!''

Epilogue

Ulysses was curled neatly in the crook of Harvey's arm, his eyes mere slits as he purred intently. His paws twitched occasionally as he dreamed of the capture of some unfortunate prey. Harvey obediently scratched beneath his chin, almost without thinking. Muffin was certainly more active. He paced the floor between the sofa and the chairs, stroking and rubbing one pair of legs after the other. The humans seemed quite oblivious to his advances as the conversation sailed back and forth above his fuzzy gray head. As a last-ditch effort, Muffin sat defiantly in the middle of the floor, with his back to everyone. He wished to give the appearance that the wall held far more interest than these big humans. He waited patiently in this position to see how long it would take until someone noticed his furry cold shoulder and tried to get his attention. Then they would see who was boss, as Muffin would cast a disinterested look over his shoulder and walk away without even a meow.

"Muffin . . ." It was Sarah, of course, who broke down first. "Muffin . . . come here, darling . . ."

Muffin cast his classic "I don't care" look, until he saw what Sarah held in her hand.

"Muffin," she teased, "I know cheese is one of your favorite snacks. Now come here to Mommy . . ."

Sarah had broken off a piece of sharply scented cheddar from the cheese-and-cracker tray. She was dangling it enticingly at Muffin's eye level. Aloofness would have to wait, as Muffin turned and trotted to Sarah. Sarah picked him up, and gave him the cheese in her lap, stroking him as he dined.

"Daddy," said Laura, "I can't believe you went out in that cold and snow and went after that horrible woman. You could have frozen to death!"

"Your father is a big boy, Laura," said her husband, Timothy. "I think he can take care of himself."

"Well, I very nearly did freeze to death," said Harvey, attempting to add to the drama. "I understand the wind chill was well below zero. A few more minutes, and I'm certain I would have at least had frostbite."

Laura shook her head as she rose to take the coffee carafe to Harvey, filling his cup. "I don't care what you say, Timothy, this whole thing scares me to death. I thought when Daddy got out of police work and into the ministry I wouldn't have to worry about him anymore.''

''I'm sorry to have frightened you, hon,'' assured Harvey. ''Believe me, it was not my idea of a fun weekend.''

''Your father did not relish what he had to do,'' said Sarah. ''He resisted being involved at the beginning. He feared for our safety, and that's why he went through with it. That's the kind of man your father has always been.''

''Sarah, dear,'' protested Harvey, ''you paint too heroic a picture.''

''Well, all the same, I would never have come out of my room if Harvey had not been there, and in control.''

''Mrs. Ashe, two of the three victims were killed in their rooms,'' Timothy pointed out with a sly grin.

''Yes, that's true,'' agreed Harvey, ''but neither of them were packing heat like your mother-in-law!''

Sarah popped Harvey on the leg, causing Ulysses to jump. Seeing nothing to be concerned about, the cat quickly drifted back into sleep.

After a few moments of gentle laughter, there seemed to be nothing left to say about the adventurous weekend. Laura, however, seemed somewhat nervous about something. Timothy poked her in the side, as if to motivate her to do something. She pushed his hand away.

"All right, Timothy," she protested, "you don't have to poke me. I'll tell them."

Harvey's attention was off of his feline, and his eyes were suddenly fixed on Laura.

"Tell us what?" he demanded in his interrogator's voice.

Laura refilled her lemonade, and took a sip.

"We've known for a few days, but we wanted to wait to tell you until after you got back from the Lodge. We didn't want to distract from your vacation."

"Vacation?" Sarah giggled sarcastically.

"Well," said Timothy, "we didn't know what was going to happen up there, after all."

"Yes, of course, we realize that," said Harvey with sudden impatience, "but get on with it. What are you talking about?"

"Well, Daddy," continued Laura, "you're going to be a grandfather!"

"Laura!" said Sarah with sudden glee. "When are you due?"

"They think the end of September, give or take a week."

Ulysses suddenly found himself alone on the couch. He stretched his legs as far as they would reach, and looked around for his pet human. Ulysses found him on the other side of the room, embracing that other human female, the one that he and Muffin (oh! the names these humans gave!) had already deduced was expecting her own litter. *Big deal*, thought Ulysses, knowing they would get over all this soon, and return their attention where it belonged: to their owners.

After the traditional hugging had subsided, a tearful Harvey led his family in a prayer for the health and safety of mother and unborn child. As he prayed he inwardly looked forward to that day when he would have the privilege of baptizing this baby. And he also looked forward to fishing trips, and Christmas presents, weekends at Grandma and Grandpa's. Sarah countered with thoughts of frilly dresses, and making doll clothes, and the old man being wrapped around the little girl's finger. Somehow Harvey and Sarah knew what each were thinking. It didn't matter, though—their lives were now changed forever, as the next generation had begun.

Too small for Laura to feel, the baby kicked his tiny foot, as he sensed the joy of his mother. In the cozy, dark warmth, he drifted back to sleep, safe and secure from the cruel world outside.